A THOUSAND MILES

A HOPE HARBOR SERIES

By: Lindsay Maves

Published by
Lindsay Maves
710 Elderberry Street.
Kaukauna, Wi 54130
(920) 279-7966
Spivy2527@yahoo.com
 ISBN: 9781546901358
Maves, Lindsay
A Thousand Miles / Lindsay Maves
cm.
Chick lit. I. Title
Printed and bound in the United States of America

<u>Grandma Ardell</u>

Not a day goes by that I don't think of you. You have touched my life more than you will ever know. I cannot wait for the day we meet again. You'll be forever in my thoughts and heart.

<u>Acknowledgement</u>

This has been my journey for over five years and I cannot thank everyone enough who has been with me on this crazy ride. It started out as a little hobby and then grew to be a dream that is now a reality. I want to thank my friends Emily Coenen, Emily Mauel, and Sara Klepps for helping me spark ideas and work with me through the nitty gritty. Thank you for Emily and Sara who helped me edit this, since I'm still working on becoming a better writer. Thank you to my husband, Lance. You have put up with me through all of this, never doubting my abilities even when I did. I want to thank my family and friends whom supported and helped me stay motivated and gave me confidence to pursue this til the end. Thank you and I love you all.

Thank you to all the beta readers:
Madison
Alicia
Jean
Jamie
Terri
Shirley

CHAPTER ONE

Eleanor had fond memories of her mother growing up. Especially when she was ten years old sitting on the hard, gray, granite countertop in the kitchen, swinging her short stubby legs, swirling the dust in the sunlight from their window that overlooked the back yard of their small, two bedroom ranch. The vibrant array of wildflowers swayed in the sticky, warm Wisconsin air, while the sweet aroma of her mother's baking filled her lungs with vanilla and caramel. Eleanor closed her long eye, fluttering her long eyelashes, smiling in pure bliss. She always looked forward to their cooking. Her grandma lived just a mile up the road. Eleanor would spend her summers sipping lemonade and eating the elegant pastries they made together. Her world revolved around them, since her father was off fighting in Iraq. He would be gone for months at a time, and she never knew when he would be home next.

"Does Daddy love your cooking?" she asked, licking the wooden spoon filled with caramel. Her mother glanced at her from the side, while continuing to whisk the batter. As Eleanor sat there with a curious look in her eyes, her mother sighed, giving in to her question.

"Yes, he said I have the best food from here to Northern Wisconsin." She turned back to the batter as she added in fresh raspberries after dredging them in flour.

"Do you know when Daddy will be home next? I miss him, I wonder if he got my last letter." Eleanor asked, gleaming with hope. Her mother's head dropped. She turned around to step in front of Eleanor, bringing her hands up to Eleanor's face and cradling it in her hands. Her mother searched into Eleanor's big green eyes wide with curiosity.

"Your Daddy passed away last month. I didn't know how to tell you my love, but your daddy was a hero, and we should always remember him that way." She wrapped Eleanor up in her arms, as her daughter rested her head on her chest. Eleanor's heart broke, but she gained a new sense of compassion for her father, a hero in her young eyes; tall in his uniform, bright red hair and those deep green eyes. She felt sadness for her mother. She hoped and prayed every night that the angels would send her father back to her.

As the years went on, times had gotten harder for their family. Abigail had trouble paying the mortgage and other utilities. Being a single parent and only working part-time at a grocery store, making a little above the minimum wage, began to be too much. She tried to thin out her budget between the bills and food. Bills took priority most times, leaving them scrapped for meals. Luckily, Eleanor's grandmother Claire would never let them starve; once a month she would take them grocery shopping to help with the necessities. Eleanor heard Abigail and Claire fight one night as she sat on the top step, peering through the wooden spokes, directing her gaze into the kitchen where they were both seated. Abigail cried when she confessed that she had no choice, but to apply to the new gentleman's club being built not far from town. No one else would hire her. Claire was happy to give Abigail money that she needed for bills, food and necessities, but Abigail refused, as she didn't want to be a burden to Claire and was determined that she could take care of her and Eleanor on her own.

"I promise I will quit once I get back on my feet. I

promise. It's not like I want to do this," Abigail cried. Eleanor's heart sunk. She didn't understand why being a dancer was so bad and didn't realize what the extent of the job position entailed until Claire told her one night after endless pleading.

Months passed after her mom was hired at the gentleman's club, making Eleanor slowly realize her mother wasn't the loveable, protective mother that she once knew. Abigail stopped doing the little things with her, reading stories, playing, and cuddling with her at night. She would apply thicker make-up, and her clothes began to show more and more of her body. She thought it was odd because Abigail never even owned lipstick before, but it seemed now she had a whole beauty salon in the bathroom. There were times when Abigail didn't come home from her shift until the next day, leaving Eleanor to fend for herself for hours on end. It forced Eleanor to learn to make her own dinner, mostly consisting of peanut butter and jelly sandwiches. Half the time she would walk a mile down the road to Claire's house for supper. On a few occasions Abigail would return in the middle of the night, waking up Eleanor as she stumble home drunk, passing out on the living room floor. She would stink of foreign substances of alcohol and heavy layer of perfume. Eleanor couldn't move her mother so she would lay a blanket over her and set a glass of water nearby. However one fateful night, her mother brought a young man home with her. They both smelled like alcohol and cigarettes. Eleanor's nose crinkled when her mom bent down to hug her. That was the first night when everything changed and Eleanor's world turned upside down by five little words her mother's male friend said, "Eleanor, let's play a game!"

Coming back to the present day, Eleanor woke up in

a cold sweat, searching frantically throughout the room, in a daze. Feeling an old weathered hand under hers, she came back to her senses, the reality of her grandmother dying. She looked up at the face that raised her after her mother dropped her on the doorstep. Her mother was convinced by her manipulative boyfriend that Eleanor was the one that ruined her life. She left soon after to go to Las Vegas with him and start a new life. Eleanor was broken when she realized that her mother was so eager to be rid of her, but she was relieved knowing that her mother's boyfriend couldn't hurt her anymore.

Eleanor watched a single tear roll down sweet Claire's leathered pale cheek, and land on her upper lip as she gazed outside, looking upon the giant weeping willow as it danced in the wind on a blustery, spring day. Her grandma's face was scattered with freckles and wrinkles in every corner. Her snow white hair glistened from the candle light, like diamonds. It brought bittersweet smile to Eleanor. Each gust of wind brought in different aromas of honeysuckle, lemon, lilacs, and peach filling the room. It brought back precious memories they shared together during warm Wisconsin summer afternoons. She smiled thinking of the old tire swing under the willow tree, and Claire pushing her. Eleanor chanted to go higher, wanting to grasp the clouds to bring them down to give to Claire. Many of their afternoons consisted of them lying out on an old soft quilt, reading excerpts from their favorite books and poems. On hot days, they would go down by the pond, swinging on the old rope, jumping off into the murky water below. Some of the best memories she had with Claire were by the old willow. It was where they could forget about the bustle of life; time stood still, and the branches would dance to the music of the wind.

Eleanor knew the sweet heavenly smells were casting a spell over Claire, giving her the same stirrings of remembrance. She couldn't tell because of the extent of damages done by the stroke that left Claire unable to communicate or function. Moments like this broke Eleanor's heart and made her realize that she would never get to hear Claire's sweet voice again, her stories about days that are long gone or her beautiful angelic singing voice during church mass. She couldn't imagine what would happen once Claire was gone. The whole small town of Wesco was a close knit community. Once everyone heard about Claire's stroke, visitors came every day. It made the big old Victorian home feel less daunting. She spent so much of her days crying it was hard to try and stay positive when the only soul she ever really loved now was hanging by a thread. The doctor said that Claire would never make a full recovery. Eleanor wanted to keep her in the hospital so they could help her in any way possible, but Claire wrote in her living will that if she became a vegetable she wanted to remain at home to die in peace. Every bone in Eleanor's body wanted to deny that Claire was dying and her chest ached at the thought.

The rain started to fall, sounding like soft drums. It had a surprisingly calming effect and the nerves that Eleanor once had slowly vanished. She snuggled up to Claire as she usually did and started to read one of their favorite romantic classics, Jane Eyre. The weather cast a hazy light over the house, making everyone in it become weary. Eleanor soon drifted off to sleep again, laying her head on Claire's shoulder, her arms wrapped around her, dreaming of the memories that they shared together. Eleanor jolted awake. Goosebumps rose on her arms and the back of her neck as she heard a strange low noise around the room.

She couldn't tell where it was coming from. A gust of wind came through the door, hitting her in the face as a voice, she swears, whispered, "I love you." Eleanor turned toward Claire who looked peacefully asleep for the first time in three weeks. Eleanor's heart jumped into her throat as her hand slowly inched toward Claire's neck, shaking once she touched her cold, soft skin. No pulse. Tears burned Eleanor's eyes as she tried remembering every detail of Claire's face. Her rounded cheek bones, her plump lips, and her frosted white hair. It felt as if all the blood had drained from Eleanor's body and she couldn't move. A pressure built up in Eleanor's lungs, making it hard to breathe. A groan escaped her mouth and she dropped to her knees next to the bed, losing control. Both of Eleanor's hands grasped Claire's cold, fragile hand. Claire was gone.

Andrew's mind was so scattered he didn't know if he was coming or going. Piles on piles of boxes of his mother's belongings took the entire space of his small red shed. He sighed in defeat, rubbing his callused hands through his shaggy, almond hair, curls falling around his face. He grunted, acknowledging along with all the items he has to do, among those was heading to the barber shop for a cut after his day was done out on the water. Andrew was a sternman on his friend Ryan's dad's lobster boat. They were a three man team, hauling over a hundred traps of succulent American Lobster in the Gulf of Maine. Andrew had been a lobsterman since he was just a freshman in high school. It helped pay for his mother's hospital bills. With her chemo, she became very sick and had to quit her job. Andrew gave up a lot of high school activities to work out on the boat with Ryan. He would be up at 4 a.m. dropping traps in the water with their signature colored buoys tied to the end. Once that was finished, they would go to another area and pull the traps up from the previous day. Andrew would measure the lobster to see if the lobsters met state regulation. Female lobsters that bear eggs would get a v-notch in the tail and be tossed backed in the water. Once all the traps were brought up, they would come back to the dock and weigh the lot. As Ryan's dad would get the price for the lot, Ryan and Andrew would race to school. After school would be spent taking his mother to an appointment or helping Ryan clean traps, to get them ready for the next morning. After Andrew finished high school, his mother was in full remission and it felt as if a weight was lifted from his chest and prayers had been answered. The next five years were happy ones, living life as they always wanted to in Hope Harbor. Tragically, Andrew could recall that dismal day. His mother came home from her yearly physical. The look in her eyes when she reached their kitchen, sitting down at the table across from him. He noticed how pale and fragile she looked. The shine in her eyes vanished.

"They found a cell in my breast, they're doing tests, but they believe the cancer returned." She whimpered and sighed in defeat. He knew she didn't have the strength to take this journey again, but he knew she must and he would be there with her every second of the way.

Andrew never regretted taking charge and the role of man of the house. For him, lobstering was a release from the pressure and responsibility. Of course on the boat he had tasks as well, but out on the water his duties felt much simpler than the ones he had to face back on land. Out on the ocean abyss, surrounded by endless blue, he could actually breathe.

Shaking his head to rid his endless thoughts, he grabbed the heaviest box and set it on the floor, grunting as he sat behind the box, folding back the cardboard. He took a deep breath, trying to calm his nerves. He knew that he should have done this a long time ago and kept putting it off, hoping magically one day he would walk into his shed and they would be all gone. It had been two years since his mother's death, and not once had he touched any of her belongings after he collected her items from the house. Pictures were scattered all throughout the box, the top one he had never seen before. It was his mother Mary standing with a taller, older lady both smiling brightly. His heart grew, gazing upon it. He truly missed his mother; she was his best friend growing up.

He exhaled sharply, flipping over to the other side of the picture to see his mother's name then the other woman's. "Claire Anderson," he muttered.

An idea hit him and soon he was frantically sorting through the other boxes to find her little black book. "Please God, let her still have the number." He prayed, flipping through the tattered old phone book.

He smiled, hopeful that this Claire Anderson could recall the good old days of his mother's life. Since she had passed, he found himself longing to find more information about his family. He wasn't sure why he wanted to know; maybe somehow it would help him face everyday life with his brother who was born with Down syndrome or maybe give insight about his father.

"Andrew, I need you to take care of Trevor, please. Promise you will never give up on him. I know it will be very hard for him, once I'm gone."

"Mother, don't say that, please don't say that."

"Just promise me."

Andrew shook away the conversation that played through his head like a broken record. He had kept that promise since that day, but he had doubts that he was doing a good job. After their mother died, Trevor stopped talking period and kept to himself. Andrew tried every way he could to get anything out of Trevor. There were only brief moments when Trevor would communicate through his expressions and actions. Andrew knew it was a start as long as Trevor wouldn't completely shut him out of his life. They were all each other had. He glanced over the picture again and knew if he didn't try and call that he would regret it. "Well...here goes nothing."

CHAPTER TWO

Surrounded by people, Eleanor couldn't help but have an overwhelming feeling that a part of her was gone. Family members gathered with one another consoling and embracing each other. Most of them said little to her, as they only associated with Eleanor when Claire was around. Eleanor never really understood why, but honestly didn't care at this point. They tolerated Eleanor this far because Claire wanted her to help out with the funeral arrangements, as stated in her living will. Eleanor sat directly in front of the casket, wanting to be close to Claire. It made the hole somewhat smaller in her heart. She couldn't help but stare at Claire's lifeless body and wonder where her soul went, if she was in heaven, watching them down below.

They laid her to rest in the casket in her favorite summer dress, blue polka dots, with her pearls around her neck. Eleanor laid her favorite flower next to Claire's shoulder, a white tulip. Every nerve and muscle in her body wanted to run up to her and shake her, hoping in some way she would wake up. Eleanor had never really lost anyone so close or dear to her. Since her mother left her at a young age and treated her so cruelly, her feelings and whatever love she had for her vanished. Eleanor could still remember the smell of cigarettes, vodka, and incense. She would hide in her room, to block out the noise of her mother yelling or crying as Dan became violent toward her, only happening when Abigail didn't bring the right drugs home. Soon after Dan started to torment Eleanor, his version of hide and seek. Only when he found Eleanor, he would torture her. Wherever she hid, he found her. He would drag Eleanor out of the room by her hair into the living room where her mom would be rocking back and forth on the couch from the hit of drug or crying because Dan had abused her. Eleanor's nightmare then would begin. He would start to kick and hit her. She would cry for Abigail to tell him to stop. She would be on her knees begging her with all the strength she had left. Abigail would get annoyed with her, "Shut up, you brat! Go to your room and stay in there...you pathetic child," She said, spitting toward Eleanor.

Eleanor shook the nasty memories from her thoughts, bringing her back to the present. It sent a spine tingling sensation deep in her bones that chilled her to the core. Eleanor hated her mother for never protecting her, but she knew somehow she would still have a tiny speck of love for her, but the pain and memories would never be erased.

The room was scattered with several flower arrangements. Some were elaborate, while others were quite simple, yet beautiful. Eleanor helped the local florist make them, as Claire would like them. Claire would have loved seeing so many flowers and the uniqueness from each arrangement. Eleanor always had a keen eye on what flowers would be paired beautifully with each other, color and smell combined as a beautiful symphony. Eleanor tried to get lost in the smell of the flora, a secret garden surrounded by multitudes of flowers as she ran through them.

"Here you go, Elle...I thought you might like something to drink." Amelia, her younger cousin, said, sitting next to her on the third step of the stairs in the grand hallway. Her honey brown hair brushed the tops of her shoulders and her bright sky-blue eyes looked clouded from crying. Her smile didn't meet her eyes as she slumped onto the step beside Eleanor. Eleanor was happy to have Amelia, for the bond they shared.

"Thanks, sweetie," she said, giving her a weak smile. Amelia placed her arm around Eleanor as Eleanor leaned her head on Amelia's shoulder and let out a sigh. It took all of Eleanor's strength not to breakdown right there.

"I can' believe she's gone..." Amelia whimpered softly, Eleanor feeling Amelia's breath on her hair. Eleanor took her hand and gently laid it on Amelia's leg, giving her a light squeeze.

"I know...what am I going to do now?"

His pulse quickened as the phone rang on the other end. It took Andrew a week to actually get the nerve to call Claire. He paced along the dock next to LUCY, the forty-eight-- foot boat that he called his second home. They called it early, after not having much luck. He ran his hand through his hair, letting out a big sigh.

"Hello?" A silky, feminine voice answered.

"Yes, um-hi, my name is Andrew Monroe and I was wondering if I could talk to Claire Anderson?" He choked the words out nervously.

He wasn't sure, but it sounded like the voice on the other end sobbed a little. Her voice became shaky as she whimpered, "I am sorry to inform you but Claire passed away two weeks ago." A lump formed in Andrew's chest.

"I am so sorry for your loss...I" he paused, not sure what to say.

"It's okay, you had no idea..." She paused. Her voice was smooth, but shaky as if she had been crying. Andrew wished he could comfort her. He hated seeing anyone in pain and having gone through losing a loved one, he had a strange pull to her. "May I ask how you knew my grandmother?" she asked.

He exhaled sharply, "I didn't. Actually, my mother did...they were friends a long time ago." He trailed off.

"Tell your mother I am deeply sorry to relay such bad news to her."

Andrew paused. "My mother passed two years ago." He replied. "I found a picture of the two of them in one of her boxes. I was hoping..."

"Oh, it's okay Andrew, I understand...I would have done the same if I was in your situation. I'm Eleanor by the way. I'm sorry I didn't tell you earlier, we have been getting a lot of phone calls today." She paused. "So...you found a picture of them?"

"Yes, a long time ago, I believe in the eighties. I am sorry if I interrupted anything." He sighed, leaning his forearm on the wooden panel of the dock, as he stared out into the vast ocean.

"You didn't, actually you..." She paused. Andrew could hear the blush through the phone that made him smile. "It's nice...to actually talk to someone really. It's weird I know, saying that I've been getting a lot of phone calls, but people   have been so short with me. It's like they're afraid to talk to me." She chuckled a little. "Well, thank you, Andrew...it's been really nice talking to you, refreshing actually." She sighed. "Unfortunately, I need to get back. You take care of yourself, Andrew. Have a good day."

Her voice had such a calming effect, he felt as if they had been friends forever. "Thank you Eleanor, it was a pleasure talking to you. I am sorry for your loss, my thoughts and prayers are with you and your family. Have a good day Eleanor. Goodbye."

"Goodbye, Andrew." He could hear her smile through the phone.

He looked at his phone after they hung up and he couldn't help but smile. The way her voice sounded on the phone, smooth as honey.

"Hey, Andrew, love...are you ready?" A voice asked breaking him from his trance. He turned to see his strikingly beautiful girlfriend of three years, Becca Taylor. He sighed as she smiled. He couldn't help but be captivated by her grace and beauty consuming everything around her. The sight of her long, gorgeous legs, and her light blonde hair sweeping across her chest, made him aroused immediately. Her smile was bright, lighting her smooth, brown eyes. A swarm of butterflies invaded his nerves making him jittery, for tonight he hoped things would change both of their lives for the better. Tonight, Andrew was going to ask Becca to be his wife.

Eleanor got off the phone with Andrew, and let her mind wander. His voice was deep, gruff, and ever so inviting. She imagined the man behind the voice: tall, dark hair, godly handsome and a rugged, chiseled face. She sighed, shivering at the image as goose bumps rose over her whole body. Her heart and mind were at war with one another. He might have a nice voice and be as beautiful as she imagined, but she couldn't get wrapped up in her heart's desires. In her mind, she was fully aware of what men, beautiful or not, had the capability of doing. She would never let any man get close enough again to take advantage of her. She had enough scars and broken bones to prove it.

"What do you mean, she gets the house?" Uncle Ron shouted, slamming his fist on the cherry oak table, making Eleanor jump out of her chair. She kept her eyes down on the table, studying the grain of the wood even though she could feel the heat from her uncle's enraged stare.

"I'm sorry sir, but that is what is stated ..." the young lawyer stated calmly, shuffling through the papers, looking unfazed on the commotion unfolding in the room.

"How dare you! You don't deserve the house! You have done nothing for this family! You are just a wench's child! Claire took you in because she felt pity on you!" he bellowed, rubbing his hand over his bald head. Those words stabbed Eleanor through the heart; Claire obviously didn't think like that.

"Sir, you do get the 1957 Cadillac Deluxe Coupe Deville..."

"I don't care about that junk car..." he rudely interrupted. Eleanor looked up glaring at him. She couldn't believe that he thought it was junk. It was his father's prized possession. Claire told her countless times how Jim would take the kids on a summer drive in the car and have picnics down by the creek.

"Sue, you're endowed with the fourteen carat ruby necklace with matching earrings. Each grandkid will receive an amount of ten thousand dollars when they turn twenty-five." He said, still ignoring the fury of her uncle who now looks like he is going to have a cornea.

Eleanor's aunt's eyes widened and she jumped up and down clapping her hands. "Yes!!" She beamed. Eleanor's stomach turned as fury rose through her bones making them boil.

"You're all unbelievable! Is this what you were all waiting for? Is this all that matters to you? Do you even care that your own mother died?" Eleanor shouted, standing up, knocking over her chair. Tears invaded her eyes, but she fought them back while her chest swelled, making it harder to breathe. Her eyes swept across the room to see their faces in shock, except her uncle who continued to glare at her.

"Oh pipe down...what is your problem? You got the bloody house!" he snapped.

"I couldn't care less what I get. I wouldn't want any of that if I could have Claire back. I was the only one who ever loved her. You're the ones that used her for her money. Ron, if you want that damn house so much you can have it: I will be out of it by the end of the week." Eleanor shouted, scooping up her papers, walking out the door as fast as she could, practically running once she got outside to the parking lot. As she walked to the car she could remember the bittersweet day when she moved in with Claire.

To Eleanor, it seemed like just one of those normal days where she sat alone in the house, her mother was God knows where. She pulled out a book that Claire snuck in for her and began reading it by the leaky window that over looked the back yard. Eleanor sighed, she actually liked this time of day when she could be alone, because sadly that is when she felt the safest; no one could hurt her.

Abigail barged into the house with Dan right behind her. "What do you think you are doing? What is this?" Abigail asked, ripping the book out of Eleanor's hand. Eleanor sunk back into the chair trying to disappear.

"Answer your mother!" Dan shouted, pushing Eleanor out of the chair. She fell onto the floor falling limp. She stared at the ground mentally preparing herself for what was going to come next.

"Doesn't matter, we won't have to deal with her much longer." Abigail laughed, throwing the book into the garbage. Eleanor raised her head slowly, watching them both laugh as they went into Abigail's bedroom.

Eleanor grew frantic, she had no idea what that even meant. Tears brimmed her eyes as she tried to fight them back. It didn't take long for them to reappear in the living room. Abigail grabbed Eleanor's arm forcing her to stand. "Come on, we are going to Grandmas." Abigail snarled.

Abigail squeezed Eleanor's arm tight, her finger nails digging painfully in her arm as she dragged her to the car, slamming the door in her face. As Abigail and Dan packed up the car, Eleanor was racking her brain as to what was going on, and as they drove the mile down the road to Claire's, Eleanor over heard her mother say, she was excited to see the bright lights and to be away from the cold weather. Confusion ran through Eleanor as she realized that their plans didn't include her. She knew right then, that her mother was leaving her.

The car sped through Claire's winding driveway, stopping abruptly at the front steps. Claire was already waiting with a mournful expression on her face. Abigail got out, going to Eleanor's side. Eleanor backed up to the other side of the car, knowing what was coming.

"Get out of the damn car, you brat!" she hollered, reaching into the car, pulling her arm as she dragged Eleanor out, tossing her onto the ground. Eleanor began to cry, she couldn't take it anymore. "Mommy, please don't leave me." Eleanor cried, gazing up at what used to be her mom. Claire rushed to Eleanor's side, consoling her. "Why are you doing this, you're throwing your life away with him!" Claire snapped, piercing her gaze into Abigail.

"You want to say that to my face, bitch?" Dan yelled from in the car. Abigail gazed at Dan then turned her head back at Claire and Eleanor. For a split second, Abigail looked vulnerable, as if a cloud was raised from her eyes.

"Get in Ab!" he bellowed, breaking her clarity. She smirked mischievously, giving them one last glance. She turned, rushed into the car and gave Dan a kiss. With that, they drove off down the road without even a backward glance.

Andrew woke in a cold sweat, panting as he looked around his bedroom. The light from his fire cast shadows on his ceiling and walls. He turned to gaze longingly at Becca. His fear of Becca rejecting him was over. She agreed to marry him last week at the docks during sunset. He tried to make it as romantic as possible and she had no idea he was going to propose. She shrieked, kissing and hugging him tightly.

Becca was there with him when his mother died,

she cared for him when he was too grief stricken to get up for a week, and consoled Andrew when Trevor shut everyone out of his life. He didn't know where he would be without her love, care, and support. She had been his anchor these past few years. He smiled just thinking of how strong their bond had grown.

"Trevor, I would like to talk to you about something important," he said as he had Trevor sit across from him at the kitchen table. Trevor's head was down, his hands folded together in front of him. "You're not in trouble, Trevor, I promise." he said reassuring him. Trevor's shoulders and arms relaxed instantly. Andrew began to relax as well. He contemplated how he was going to tell Trevor that he was going to propose to Becca.

"Becca has been there for us so much these past couple years after Mom died. I know you like her, Trevor, even though at times I can tell she can be a bit too much for you." He paused, looking at Trevor's expression change, becoming more curious. "I love Becca, Trevor. I want her to be a part of our lives more permanently." Trevor's eyes darkened as they widened. "I want to ask her to marry me." Andrew stated, not expecting Trevor's reaction, as he pounded his fist on the table, alarming Andrew. Trevor's breathing increase, making Andrew afraid that he would have a panic attack. Andrew rushed to Trevor's side, slowly placing his hand on his shoulder. Trevor shrugged Andrew's hand away. Andrew kneeled down next to Trevor, trying to make eye contact with him.

"Please, Trevor, don't shut me out." Andrew cooed, placing his hand onto Trevor's shoulder, this time Trevor didn't fight him. Andrew could feel Trevor's shoulders shake as if he was crying. "Trevor, please don't cry. I promise things won't change around here. She can never replace Mom, but I love Becca," Andrew stated as Trevor looked at him. Andrew took his other hand and brushed Trevor's short brown hair back. Andrew could see his same blue eyes stare back at him, with tears flowing down Trevor's cheeks. It felt like a knife through Andrew's heart. He stared back at Trevor as tears threatened to escape his own eyes. He could feel Trevor's gaze invading his soul. Andrew held his breath, hoping that Trevor would just smile and be okay with the idea. As if he read Andrew's thought, Trevor frowned and shook his head. Andrew's whole body slumped.

"Can you at least think about it, for me?" Andrew begged. Trevor nodded once as he dropped Andrew's hand off his shoulder. Trevor got up from the table and went into his room. Andrew dropped to the floor, putting his head into his hands. He couldn't fight back the tears anymore. Days like this, he wished his mother could be here. Trevor would be his normal self and their world would be happy and peaceful once more.

Rubbing his eyes, clearing his thoughts, Andrew slowly got out of bed, doing his best not to wake Becca. He put on his slippers and quietly slipped out the door. He headed down the hall to the last door on the left. He quietly opened the door to gaze upon his brother as he slept. He couldn't help but grin. His brother was surrounded by Superman merchandise from bed sheets to pajamas, and stuffed toys. His room had deep sea blue walls and white ceiling. The walls neatly displayed posters of medieval knights, superman, and dinosaurs. Andrew always did his best to please his brother, making sure he was happy and had every opportunity available.

Before their mother died, they had been somewhat

close. Andrew was more of a father figure to Trevor than a brother, and that didn't change after their mother died. He wished he could be more of a brother than a father. Maybe one day he hoped, but he never regretted it; he would do anything for Trevor. He loved his brother dearly, he thought as he leaned his head back on the white molded door frame, sighing. More than anything, he prayed that his brother would one day talk again. He missed their conversations, jokes, and Trevor's laughs. He was in awe of how Trevor saw the world and missed how he would explain it to Andrew; it captivated and inspired him to try to look at the world differently as well. It didn't matter how bad Andrew's day was, once Trevor smiled and giggled, it was the only thing that made it better.

After a couple of minutes passed, Andrew sluggishly headed back to bedroom where he got dressed for work. As he got ready, his mind flashed back to the strangest dream that woke him up in the first place. In his dream he was consumed by cold, wet dark darkness... He panicked when he thought he was dying, the darkness taking deeper. He desperately tried to swim toward the light shining above. As he moved toward the light, a voice started to whisper. He couldn't make it out at first, but then it got louder and louder. As much as he tried, he couldn't figure out whose voice pleaded, "Andrew...I love you. Come back to us."

He walked down the pier to the boat where Ryan was waiting for him. He tried to analyze the hidden message behind the dream. His mind raced and he couldn't help feel that this dream mattered in some way. But whose voice was that?

CHAPTER THREE

Opening up the attic door, she was bombarded with cobwebs and dust. She coughed, wiping the webs out of her face, quickly turning on the flash light. After the scene in the lawyer's office, the attorney called her back the next day saying that he wasn't done talking to her about the will settlement. She reluctantly went back and when she got there the man who witnessed her estranged family's behavior had a look of sympathy on his face.

"I'm sorry about yesterday with my family, I..." she trailed off looking at the ground. He coughed, making her look up at him.

He shook his head. "No need. They were the ones that were cruel, not you. I am sorry you have to go through this. Here, this is for you." he said, handing her a small manila envelope.

"What is this?" Eleanor questioned, feeling the velvety texture of the envelope in her hands.

"A letter your grandma left you. Read it once you

get home."

Which lead her to the attic. According to the letter, Claire had left a chest of memorable family heirlooms in there and wanted Eleanor to have it.

"My dearest Ellie,
Words cannot express how much joy you brought to my life. When your mom left, I was unsure if I could raise another child again, but you have always been different from other girls your age, more mature and with such a kind soul. You reminded me of myself when I was younger; always looking at the world with a curious and vivid mind. Then you grew into a beautiful woman that I couldn't be more proud of. Thank you for filling my life with a tremendous amount of love and laughter. I love you now and forever.
Claire."

There is a chest up in the attic that I want you to have when I leave this earth. In the chest are my dearest belongings. I want you to have everything in that chest and cherish it for the rest of your life. I have a feeling that one day you might need some of the items in that chest so take great care of them. Along with this I am entitling you to my trust fund I have set up. I hope with this, you seek out your wildest dream Ellie. I love you with all my heart. Please never forget.
Love, Claire."
She held the letter tightly to her chest, blinking through the tears that rolled down her face. She walked through the attic looking for the chest. She found it by the window overlooking the willow in the background. She couldn't grasp the elegance of the chest. It was

medium sized with elaborate hinges and designs on the front and on the border around the top. The wood was either cedar or oak and the color was rich red wine. Luckily it didn't have a lock on it. She bent down in front of it, brushing off the layers of dust and slowly opened the top.

Once opened, there was a big plastic bag. She pulled out the bag to find Claire's wedding dress. She pulled the dress out of the bag and gasped in awe at the delicacy of the design. It was a knee length, white satin beaded lace dress with an A-line neckline. She held it up to her and looked into the floor length mirror next to her. She smiled with tears in her eyes once more. It was simple and elegant and looked like a perfect fit. Eleanor knew if she got married one day that this would be her dress. She carefully placed it back in the bag, reaching back into the chest to find old pictures of her ancestors and baby pictures of her grandma and mother.

In the way bottom was a small blue velvet box. She opened it to see what she assumed was Claire's engagement ring. A sterling silver skyline ring with an extensive sapphire lay in a halo of diamonds. She carefully put it on her ring figure, again perfect fit. She held her hand out to see it in the light from the window. The sapphire burst like waves in an ocean storm. She caressed each gem, thinking it was all a dream. She looked back down in the chest thinking it was empty but there was a card left. She opened the letter to see that it was from a woman named Mary. She was wishing Claire to come back to Maine soon. Then there was a picture of them standing in front of a house together with a sold sign in the back. Eleanor thought they must have lived together at some point. She noticed Mary holding onto a small baby, a glimmer flickering in her head. "Was this

Andrew and his mother?" Eleanor thought, excited at the aspect of it. She knew that once she moved out of the house that she would be heading to Maine. She had to find out more about Mary and the life that Claire led in Maine. A small part of her heart jumped at the mere thought of finally meeting Andrew. Could this be what her grandmother is leading her to?

Andrew couldn't shake the dream out of his head. During the past week he had the dream twice, resulting in him waking up in a cold sweat. It also didn't help that he kept finding more and more information about how Claire and his mother related to one another. It almost became an obsession. After he got back from work with Ryan, he would go straight to his shed and look through the boxes. He didn't want to be away from Trevor too long though so he started having Trevor help look through the boxes with him, making it into a game.

As they looked through the boxes, when one found something interesting the other one would shout...Well, Trevor would just raise his hand. Andrew found letters between Mary and Claire and he would read them out loud. Trevor would just sit content next to Andrew looking so curious and intrigued. With the help of Trevor, he found out that Claire and Mary were childhood friends that grew up next door together, but Claire moved to Wisconsin when she was ten with her family. Once she turned eighteen Claire moved back to Maine and found a place with Mary. He still couldn't figure out though why Claire moved back to Wisconsin after that. His mother never mentioned a Claire growing up. His worst fear was that they had a falling out or a disagreement that tore their friendship apart.

Andrew and Trevor's eyes met after finding the latest letter. Andrew put his hand on Trevor's shoulder, as he read it out loud.

"I miss her too, Trev. We've only got each other now. I am going to do my best by you, okay?" Tears formed in his eyes, "I love you, you know that right?"

Trevor looked a moment longer into Andrews's eyes studying Andrew with his piercing blue eyes that matched Andrew's. Trevor placed his hand on top of Andrews; smiling and nodding. Andrew's smile grew wider.

"Thank you, buddy. I know it hasn't been easy for you, but I will always be here for you, okay." Trevor squeezed Andrew's hand again. Andrew was ecstatic, it was the one of the rare moments that Trevor showed Andrew how he felt.

They settled back inside after spending a few hours in the shed, so Trevor could take his afternoon nap. Andrew headed to the patio to let his mind and heart breathe. He was speechless from the interaction he had with Trevor earlier.

Now his mind went back to his haunted dreams with the mysterious woman's voice. The dream plagued his mind and the scene left a hunger in his heart. He was baffled at his strong attachment to the woman in the dream but couldn't understand why. Could it just be the intensity of the dream itself that lured him to her?

"There you are! I have been looking all over for you," Becca exclaimed, making him jump as he turned around to her. She cocked her head, looking surprised. "I'm sorry I didn't mean to scare you." She walked up to him, wrapping her arms around his biceps, leaning her head on his shoulder, looking up at him.

"It's okay, I was just thinking," he mumbled, looking down at her, capturing the radiant brown in her eyes.

"About what?" she asked.

"Trevor. We had an interaction today. It was simply wonderful." He smiled.

"That is awesome love, I am so happy for you." She leaned up, kissing his cheek, his growing stubble prickling her lips. "Are we still on for tonight? There is something I would like to discuss with you."

Andrew raised his eyebrow, confused. "About?"

She pulled away, smacking his arm, giggling. "About the wedding, silly. You do remember proposing to me, right?"

He chuckled nervously, "Oh...yeah, right. How could I forget? Sure, that would be great."

"Well I've got to head home to get ready. Daddy wants to take me to the car dealership out in Wiscasset. I am hoping for a Range Rover." She smiled brightly, giving him one last kiss then walking out the door without as much as a goodbye. Andrew scowled as he watched her walk away.

Sometimes Andrew wondered about Becca. She was rich, that much was obvious, but he couldn't understand why her family, especially her father, seemed to loath him. Maybe he was still trying to buy her back, so she didn't leave her daddy to be with a poor fisherman. Little did anyone know; that Andrew was, in fact, quite the opposite. He was left with some money from his mother's death, but for the most part, he was saving all his overtime from work. He wanted to use it for Trevor, when or if he wanted to go to college. Andrew didn't see the importance of money as others did. Surely Becca didn't love him for his money, because as far as she was concerned, he didn't have any.

Andrew pulled out the phone to look at the time and then thought to himself, "Why don't I call Eleanor...see how she is doing." A tiny part of him actually wanted to hear her voice again, and before he knew what he was doing the phone was ringing.

"Hello?"

"Hi, is Eleanor there?"

The voice on the other end let out a mad huff and bellowed, "No, she doesn't live here anymore!"

"May I ask where she moved to?" Andrew asked politely.

"Don't know and honestly don't care," he bellowed hanging up the phone.

Andrew closed his phone and grimaced. Maybe it's a good thing she left, but he couldn't help but wonder where she moved. His heart sunk a little knowing that he would most likely never get to hear her voice again. He only prayed that wherever she was, she was safe from harm and healing from the pain. He went back inside the house after the spring air began to chill and the sun set. He slumped on the couch and his eyes found the picture of his mother and Claire.

He whispered, "Claire, please let Eleanor be okay."

One of the hardest decisions Eleanor ever had to face was choosing whether to walk away or try harder. She knew there was no way she could try harder with her family. Her family obviously wanted nothing to do with her based on her mother's life choices. It took all of

Eleanor's might to walk away from the house she called home for the last eighteen years, but she did. A bittersweet feeling swept over her body as she drove down the dirt road to the main highway. Claire's engagement ring hung on a silver platinum necklace dangling from her neck. The rays from the sun hitting the diamonds made the inside of the car gleam with rainbows. She clutched the necklace tight in her hand, holding it close to her heart.

She glanced back in the rearview mirror one last time, remembering all the fond memories she once shared there. She couldn't explain the eerie darkness that seemed to fall on the house as she moved further away from it. There was no point going back now; she had nothing to go back to.

It was going to be a long haul to Hope Harbor, Maine. Eleanor's body hummed with excitement and fear. Once she saw the letters, she thought of nothing else. Everything now was crammed in the back of her dependable Volvo 240 Wagon. That was another item that was left in the will, and apparently the only thing that her uncle didn't care about at all.

"It's a piece of shit, have fun driving it!" He laughed, stomach jiggling in the chair.

She didn't mind. It was a reliable car. It made her a little lightheaded to think she was going to start all over again on her own in a new state where she didn't know anyone. Well, there was one person- Andrew. She wasn't sure if he still lived there and she barely knew him. She knew above anything else, that she was meant to find him.

Driving on HWY 1, anticipation flowed through her body like a current, filling her with the desire to step on the gas. The sun started to rise and cast a magnificent array of colors in the sky. Her heart pounded in her chest, her skin felt alive. The weight of what happened almost a month ago was lifted from her like a cloud, floating out the window and heading toward the sky. Trees now surrounded her vehicle, making the ocean seem far away. She pushed on, making her old car speed a little faster, wanting to be near the sound of crashing waves.

She headed down a street where she found multitudes of docks. She quickly parked and rushed out, running to the nearest one. Her heart hummed louder in her chest. She pushed herself faster, reaching the end of the dock, collapsing to her knees. She looked up to the sky, as if to search for a clue. Some answer to confirm this was what she was meant to do. A tear fell upon the dock. She let everything go, all the pain and emotion that she had built up inside her for so long. She rocked on her knees as she cradled her head in her hands, pouring her heart out to the endless water ahead. The smell of the sea mist overwhelmed her, the tiny beads kissing her skin. Her hair fell free from the tie that kept it in place and began to dance wild in the wind, wrapping around her. She leaned back looking up toward the sky again as she closed her eyes, letting out a sigh. It felt as if a huge boulder left her shoulders, the darkness in her eyes brighter. She felt finally able to breathe in life again.

She wasn't sure just how long she was in that position. She quickly got up from her knees, noticing the wood grain had etched in her skin. She brushed off her shorts and looked out onto the water once more. The sun rose higher now dancing upon the waves in a forbidden tango. Colors of blue, purple, and white cascaded over the surface of the water. Eleanor smiled out over the water and let out a small laugh. For the first time since

Claire was gone, she felt free.

CHAPTER FOUR

Reality set in a few days later when Eleanor felt frantic as she tried to find a job around the small area of Hope Harbor. She knew today had to be the day to find one. She used a part of her savings to rent out a motel till she found a job. She didn't want to have to use the money she got from Claire just yet. She planned on buying a small cottage she fell in love with.

The small, light green cottage was nestled in a wooded patch on top of a hill. It was pretty worn down; the white shutters worn and tattered. There were two big bushes in the front of the house beneath the two big windows. They were quite over grown and half dead. A knee height brick wall was built in the front of the house, with different misshapen stones. It blocked the yard from the sidewalk and some of the mortar and brick started to crumble at a touch. It was at a good price; her mind thought of countless possibilities and plans to change the cottage into her future home. She called the realtor that had posted the sign and set up a meeting. She wanted the house as soon as possible. Her body tingled with excitement. This cottage needed her as much as she needed it.

That afternoon, she walked down the street and noticed a small floral shop with a hiring sign in the window. It had white panels with huge windows in the front. On the roof were dozen of bushes with a variety of colors that added a homey feel. Eleanor grinned and quickly headed inside. People scattered throughout the store. The cashier section had an array of flower arrangements and off to the side was a section of sweets and fudge. Another wall had a table with shelves behind it, where the specialist made the color arrangements. It had an array of different styles and colors of vases. It looked like an organized work station. She pictured herself working back there, making exquisite bouquets like the ones that she used to make back home.

She walked up to a stunning woman with fiery red hair, pulled back into messy pony tail. The woman appeared to be around Eleanor's age. When their eyes met, Eleanor couldn't help but notice how the woman's brown eyes shimmered from the sunlight and freckles were scattered all over her face. A closer look at the woman's face and Eleanor could see she looked quite tired. The woman smiled and Eleanor was next in line.

"Hi, how may I help you?"

"Hi, my name is Eleanor Welsh. I am new to this area and saw your hiring sign in the window. I would like to have an application please."

The woman's eyes widened and she looked relieved. "Hi, I am Rachel, the manager for Beauty Within Floral Boutique. Do you have any experience and knowledge about flowers?"

Eleanor nodded, "Yes, My grandma and I used to have our own business in our small town back home."

Rachel didn't say anything. She squinted and

studied Eleanor. She bit the bottom of her lip, and then quickly smiled. "Here's the thing. We are extremely busy right now and could use all the help we can get. We have a wedding today and our team hasn't finished making the arrangements. You can help out today and by the end of the night I will determine whether you get the job or not, deal?"

"Deal!" Eleanor grinned, shaking hands.

"Okay, head in the back and you will find Benjamin. He will show you what to do from there." Rachel instructed, pointing Eleanor in the right direction. Eleanor was relieved that Rachel didn't see her stiffen. Eleanor wasn't around men much and she made an effort to keep it that way.

"Why, hello there, beautiful! You must be Eleanor." A man around Eleanor's age smiled brightly. The sides of his eyes crinkled, while his hazelnut eyes glowed under the fluorescent lights.

She gulped loudly, her body stiffening again. Her eyes grew wide and she became leery. "Hi," Eleanor mumbled. Her heart instructed her not to worry. Her mind warned her that she couldn't be too careful around new men. She tried to quiet the argument that was going on between them. She walked toward him but kept her distance. He held out his hand for her to shake. She started to inwardly panic. She quickly raised her hand, barely touching his, shook it once then dropped it, tucking her own hand back into her pocket.

Benjamin stared at her for a moment puzzled, then shrugged as he turned back to the arrangement he was working on. He appeared so focused and his hands delicately touched the flowers, arranging them in the right places. Eleanor couldn't help but be fascinated with his process, absorbing all the information.

"Why don't you add some soft, pink roses with the purple Hydrangeas? They would complement each other really well." She mumbled quietly, "I mean, if they are in the wedding colors of course."

He set down the flower he was cutting and turned to look at her, studying her again. He turned back to the arrangement he started putting together and just shook his head. She was afraid that he didn't like her critiquing his work but he turned to her and smiled. "You have a very good eye, I hadn't thought about that, but I think that would look very nice! Thank you." He smiled. Eleanor's shoulders relaxed a bit. She knew with starting over, she had to learn to trust men again. Her past left a mark on her heart that never fully healed and scars on her body that would make it hard for her to ever forget. She unconsciously held her arm where one of the many cigarette burns etched into her body. She shook her head trying to clear her mind and began doing the same as Benjamin, still keeping a distance between them. Being in the same room was even a big step for her-especially since they were alone.

While they worked, he would glance over at her process and study her work. She would look when he did, their eyes meeting. He would smile then go back to work. Eleanor couldn't deny that Benjamin was an attractive man. He had messy, sandy brown hair, big chestnut eyes, rounded cheekbones, a rounded chin, and a big smile.

"These are amazing! Eleanor, did you create these?" Rachel shrieked, walking into the room after a few hours, quickly rotating the vases to look at the arrangements. Eleanor's blush deepened.

"Yes, I thought I would just arrange them a little differently. I hope you don't mind."

"Mind? These are incredible! Eleanor, you're hired! Pay starting today, can you stay till close?" Rachel pleaded, eyes looking big. Eleanor smiled gratefully. How could she have gotten so lucky doing something she loved so much?

Rachel ran up and hugged Eleanor tightly, "You are such a blessing to us. I thought we would be ruined if we didn't find someone soon!"

Eleanor was at a loss for words for a moment; she couldn't believe that Rachel hardly knew her but was so open and welcoming. Eleanor smiled, tears forming in her eyes, trying her best not to cry. "I would love too."

"Oh honey, I didn't mean to make you cry." Rachel rubbed Eleanor's back. Benjamin looked at her concerned. "Are you okay?"

Eleanor let out a chuckle, "Yes."

"Why don't you go out back to the green house and get some fresh air. There are plants back there that need to be watered." Rachel smiled softly. Eleanor nodded walking toward the door. She turned back around smiling, "Thank you. Thank you for everything."

Rachel smiled brightly, "You're very welcome darling, and thank you for being our savior today." Benjamin nodded smiling warmly at her as she blushed quickly walking away.

Eleanor turned around and headed outside to one of the many greenhouses on the property. She had no idea the shop had such a large area. She headed to the one closest to the store, grabbing an apron and watering can, and began to water the abundance of African marigolds, pansies, pink scarlet flax, and Chinese forget-me-nots. She was moved by the lavish colors and inviting smells. At the end of the greenhouse, there was a younger man, over by one of the flowers beds, talking to it. Eleanor froze wondering whether he was really supposed to be there. He turned around, surprised to see her standing there. Smiling, he began to walk toward her. Her muscles locking up, she focused on the flowers before her hoping that he would just walk by without any conversation; this day was already draining. She pushed on carefully, watering each and every pot accordingly. The boy walked up to her; she could feel his gaze on her. The air became alive, the colors of the flowers illuminating all around her. She slowly turned up to look in his soft, warm, China blue eyes. They had an instant calming effect and she couldn't help but relax her shoulders. She noticed he wasn't like most boys in their twenties. He smiled sweetly at her.

"I'm Trevor," he said quietly, as he continued to smile at her. His chubby cheeks pushed up high, making his eyes become slits and two dimples formed on each side of his mouth.

"Hi, I'm Eleanor," she said, giving him a halfhearted smile. "Is there something I can do for you?" she asked.

"I wanted to pick up some flowers for my mom." he mumbled, looking down at the flower.

"Oh that's so nice of you. What is her favorite flower?" She turned, looking over the variety of flowers.

"White tulips." He grinned, turning to look at her.

Eleanor's eyes lit up, smiling at Trevor excitedly, "Well it just so happens that I made some flower bouquets with white tulips, if you would like to see them?"

"I would like that." He smiled back, but it didn't reach his eyes. Trevor followed Eleanor back to the store toward the back where they made the arrangements.

"Wait here," she replied, quickly going into the back of the store where she grabbed a small vase full of white tulips and soft pink carnations.

"Here, this is on me. I hope your mother likes it as much as I enjoyed making them." She grinned, gently putting it in his hands.

He looked down at the vase, and then back up at her with a growing sense of sadness. Her heart swelled in her chest as she saw the pain in his eyes. "I think she will."

"Have you seen Trevor?" Andrew frantically asked Rachel catching her outside the store, running from his truck. He got a distraught phone call from his neighbor, Elizabeth, who watched Trevor every morning while Andrew was out on the water. Trevor had made it a habit of running from home lately, always ending up at one place, the flower shop.

She raised an eye brow looking, confused. "Yeah, he's with Eleanor, our new employee." She saw his expression, then sighed, "He ran away again, didn't he?"

Andrew let out a groan, rubbing his hand through his hair, feeling his anger rise. "I hope he isn't causing any havoc. Wait-he is with someone?" he asked as his body froze.

Andrew turned to head into the store with Rachel when he stopped dead in his tracks as he saw Trevor giggling with a mysterious woman. Trevor looked up to see Andrew. He gave Eleanor back the vase of flowers, slowly walking toward Andrew looking ashamed. She looked up curiously at Andrew. Her eyes got wide and she involuntarily took a step back when she saw him, her body freezing almost as a small child afraid of the monster under the bed, making herself smaller.

Andrew tried not to stare at Eleanor, but it was hard when her beauty flowed throughout the whole store. Wave upon wave of electricity crashed into his chest making it ache. Yet, she looked terrified of him.

"Trevor, you had me and Elizabeth worried sick about you," he said, walking up putting his hand on Trevor's shoulder. He bent down to Trevor's level, "I'm not mad at you, buddy, you just scared us, okay? Especially Elizabeth...she sounded terribly frightened when she called me. You know how fragile she is, bud, " he said, pleading with Trevor, hoping to make some contact with him. Trevor raised his head up to look at Andrew. Andrew's heart sunk to see Trevor's eyes sadden, but Trevor gave him a smirk, which was a good sign in Andrew's book.

"Sorry, it's my fault, we met in the greenhouse and got to talking. I wanted..." She started to say, folding her hands together in front of her looking down at the ground, as her voice trailed off.

"Wait--what? He spoke to you?" Andrew asked, choking out his words as he peered down at Trevor, who now avoided his gaze. His tone was deeper and harsher than he meant it to sound. What made her so special that Trevor could open up to a complete stranger?

"Umm...yes?" she asked, confused. Andrew looked at Trevor, who was still staring at the ground, then back up to Eleanor.

"He hasn't talked to anyone since our mother died," he explained, still keeping his gaze down at Trevor. She brought a hand up to her mouth and gasped.

"I am sorry for your loss, I didn't know." She paused, glancing down quickly at her hands that were intertwined with one another. Her knuckles were white as she was. She took in a deep breath, keeping her eyes on the floor, but lingered at his boots. He wanted to shout at her that his eyes were up here. He disliked when people didn't make eye contact when they spoke. He believed it was disrespectful for both parties.

"I wanted to give him these flowers for her," she exclaimed, quietly. She appeared to be trying to look at anything except for him. Andrew looked at the vase of flowers in her hand and couldn't deny that they were beautiful. "We can't accept those."

She looked at the vase of flowers, baffled studying the arrangement. "Why not?"

Andrew's anger rose, "We don't want your pity," he said regretting the words as soon as they came out of his mouth. He shut his eyes tightly, grimacing as he mentally kicked himself in the ass. He opened his eyes to notice her shoulders drooped, mouth gaped and her eyes widened, obviously hurt. Trevor stepped away from Andrew glaring up at him, anger spread across his face. Trevor looked away from Andrew in disgust and walked up to Eleanor and whispered in her ear. He took her hand, giving it a light squeeze as he looked into her eyes. She looked brittle to the touch. Trevor let go of her hand and walked back to Andrew, still glaring at him.

"Andrew, I don't think that..." Rachel chimed in. Andrew forgot that Rachel was standing behind him. Andrew put his hand up cutting her off as he turned to look at her with pleading eyes. She only nodded and backed away.

"Let's go." Andrew sighed, putting his hand back on Trevor's shoulder as they walked out of the store. He knew he should have handled himself better, but envy over took him. He made it worse when he accused her of taking pity. If only his mother could see him now. He knew she would be cursing him out for being so rude to a lady. As his foot hit the pavement, it echoed with the pounding of his heart. He got into the truck, slamming the door a little louder than necessary.

Trevor started out the window as they drove home. Andrew's mind contemplated the previous events. He knew he would have to apologize not just to Rachel, but to Eleanor as well. Eleanor... a light bulb clicked in his head. Why didn't he think about it before! Her voice sounded familiar, but he was so wrapped up he didn't really pay attention to it. Could it really be her? He was surprised that he recognized her voice after so long. He agreed to himself that the only way he would know for sure was to go back to the shop, but would she be willing to see him?

CHAPTER FIVE

Eleanor's phone rang as she walked to work on a brisk Tuesday morning. She glanced at her phone, a smile spreading across her face.

"Amelia, how are you?" Eleanor asked excitedly walking down the sidewalk enjoying the sound of the birds in the trees.

"I am doing well, I miss you. Where are you?" Amelia asked.

"You will never guess... Maine!" Eleanor exclaimed. "I just bought my own little cottage on top of a hill looking over the bay and I have a job at a florist shop."

Amelia gasped, "This is so amazing! I am happy for you Elle." She paused. "I'm sorry for what my dad said to you. He had no right."

Eleanor grimaced as she recalled that day, but shrugged her shoulders as she crossed the street walking in front of a cute, white house. A family played in the front yard happily, for a moment Eleanor's heart ached. Would she ever be ready to overcome her fear of men so she might have a chance to have her own family one day? She knew she wanted one. Her heart wanted her to be in love and to be swept off her feet. It was her mind that needed more convincing.

"It is in the past... Hey, maybe one day you can come visit and stay with me for a while." Eleanor suggested, wanting nothing more than to see her dear cousin again.

Amelia smiled through the phone, "There would be nothing I would love to do more. Maybe even this fall! I have to run but please keep in touch, Elle. I love you."

Eleanor's heart swelled. "I will Amelia, I love you too. Bye sweetie." It was something she needed to hear and coming from her cousin meant the world to her. She knew someone out there, at least one person loved her.

The door chimed as Eleanor stood on the top rung of the ladder hanging up sale posters for their Easter blow out.

"I will be right there, one second please." she called out as she struggled to put the tack in the wood. She grunted, using as much strength as she could muster to push it in with her palm. Sighing in relief, she wiped her forehead, scattered with pebbles of sweat.

"No problem," said the guest in a deep masculine voice, echoing through her body. She knew that voice; it haunted her dreams the past week. Her pulse and breathing quickened just thinking of those raging blue eyes that cast a hole in her heart. She knew it was Andrew from the day they first met in the floral shop. She wished this time she could control her fear that got the best of her last time. She found him greatly attractive, except the arrogant jerk part. Definitely not the same person she talked to on the phone.

She tipped her head over slightly to see him, making the ladder tilt. She let out a yelp as the ladder started to fall. Andrew caught it before it went any further.

"You okay?" he asked voice low and husky, making her heart flutter. She looked into his light blue eyes and froze at the beauty they captured. His eyes were like ocean waves, colliding with each other during a fierce storm. Her heart jumped into her throat, pulsing through her whole body, and for a second she couldn't say anything. All she could hear was her heart beating.

Something clicked in her mind once the aroma of his cologne overwhelmed her senses. Flashbacks of her nightmares came flooding into her mind. She used all her power to push him away, standing a couple feet away from him. She took deep breaths trying to control her frantic heart. She ran her fingers through her hair, trying to think about anything but him. She looked at the floor, only seeing his steel toe boots in view. She noticed how dirty and worn they were.

"You don't look very well, would you like some water?" Andrew asked sounding concerned, taking a step closer to her.

She took a step back, still looking at the ground. She knew if she looked into his eyes, it would be the end of her.

"That's okay, I can get it myself. I don't want your sympathy." She snapped, walking behind the counter grabbing her mug of tea. She took a sip of it, hoping it would calm her nerves.

She was aware of his features from their first meeting, but it didn't take effect, until she saw him stand before her, then she was blind-sided. He appeared to be in his late twenties, looking as if he just got done with work. He wore tattered jeans and a dirty plaid button-- down shirt with the two buttons undone, showing off his dark brown chest hair. He had a chiseled jaw, high sharp cheek bones, and brooding eyebrows, with an almond chestnut brown hair that was disheveled. A hint of copper in his beard made his light blue eyes shine. Honestly, she had never seen someone so statuesque in all her life.

She set down the tea, turning slowly around to face him. Andrew gazed at her. His piercing china-blue eyes had drops of a golden hue; it made her thighs tingle. She wasn't used to having these feelings for any man. It made her feel vulnerable.

He leaned on the table, placing his huge rugged hands on the counter top. "Eleanor, I am sorry for how I acted." He sighed, trying to get her to look at him.

"I don't know if I can believe you," she snapped, as she stared at the paperwork in front of her, ignoring him until the scent of his musk consuming her lungs once more.

He grunted. "I am sorry. I know I don't even know you and I misjudged you...the thing is... I was jealous of you," he admitted frustrated, his hands balling up into a fist, looking down at the counter. She was shocked by him admitting it.

"Me...why?" she asked looking at him in bewilderment.

"Trevor..." he exclaimed. "I have been trying to get him to speak for over a year. Then you come along...I walk in to see you smiling and laughing with each other. I would give anything to have that with him. It was like a knife in my heart. I am sorry that I took that out on you."

He suddenly smiled, "It's really you, isn't it? Claire's granddaughter, it's actually you!" He beamed standing up, and walked around the counter, standing close to her.

She nodded as her eyes widened as she backed up into the wall. She put her hand out urging him not to come any closer. "Please, don't." He stopped as he cocked his head confused, but reluctantly started to back away. Just standing that close to him, she could feel the heat coming off of him. It swarmed her body. The feeling made her anxious again, but she couldn't deny that she liked it. "I knew it was you the whole time...as soon as I saw you," she said letting out a nervous chuckle, and you look like your mother."

"Wait...How did you know-?" he asked, raising his eyebrow.

Eleanor pulled an envelope out of her back pocket. She'd kept it with her since arriving in Maine, hoping to encounter him, so she could show him. She looked at it, and then glanced up at him. She slowly handed it to him, highly aware that her hand was shaking horribly. When he reached for the picture, he instead grabbed her hand. She gasped and panic spread into her veins. She tried to pull her hand away, but he warmly wrapped his strong, massive hand tighter around hers. It made hers feel so much smaller and brittle. Electricity shot up her arm, sending a shooting prickling sensation throughout her whole body. She wanted to relax like she did when Trevor touched her.

"Eleanor..." he pleaded. After a coruscating moment, she glanced up at him, pleading with her eyes to let her go.

"Please..." she whispered, eyes brimming with tears as she looked back down at their hands once more. It was too much for her to handle at the moment and she felt as if she wanted to combust right there. He dropped her hand finally, taking the picture. She glanced up at him, noticing his face was almost unreadable, but she could sense he was hurt in some way. He didn't say anything, but she knew he didn't have to. Eleanor watched Andrew look at the picture, then flipping it to the back, reading the letter attached. He smirked as he read it.

"Thank you for showing me this," he said, continuing to stare at the picture. "Do you think maybe sometime we could...?" he paused, letting out a nervous cough. "I mean, I would like to show you some things I have found that relates to my mom and your grandma, if you're up for it?" he asked, handing back the picture. Eleanor smiled weakly at him. Her first impression of him definitely changed from their first encounter. Everything that she once thought he was, slowly vanished. She wanted to gain more opportunities to see if that was really true. She gulped loudly, knowing that meant spending more time with him. She knew that her life depended on pushing forward, no matter how hard that was going to be. The perfect person to maybe help nudge her when she needed it the most was standing right in front of her.

"Sure, that would be nice." She smiled. His eyes lit up and once again she was struck by his beauty. He gave her his number and address and told her to call him when she knew her schedule. He headed for the door, but stopped to look at her one last time as he smiled, showing his dimples then continued to walked out the door. She knew right then she was in trouble; falling for him. There was only one question; was she brave enough to let her heart take over?

Andrew paced back and forth in his living room, waiting for Eleanor to show up. He didn't understand why he was so nervous. For crying out loud he was engaged! Whenever those fiery hazel eyes and bright smile popped into his mind, a swarm of butterflies rushed in his stomach.

"Get a hold of yourself..." He muttered to himself as he ran his hand through his shaggy, curly hair. He didn't want to admit to himself that he had a slight attraction-- hell not a slight attraction, a full on attraction to Eleanor. The one thing that really bothered him was the way her body tensed up whenever he was near her, even though that didn't apply to Trevor. He just couldn't figure her out and he was usually able to read people well. It was almost like she had a wall built around her, made him more determined to find out why.

A knock interrupted his thoughts. He opened the door, getting a blast of warm vanilla and strawberry fragrance, knocking him off his feet. Eleanor smiled shyly at him; her cheeks flushed as their eyes met. She wore simple faded jeans and a t-shirt. Her rich, dark, auburn hair swayed perfectly on her ample bosoms. He quickly averted his eyes once they lingered there, making his face become warm.

"Hello." She smiled.

He gulped, "Hi, um please come in." He gestured moving aside to let her through. She walked in, taking in the sight of the house. She turned back toward him unexpectedly, running right into his chest. He let out an involuntary groan making Eleanor quickly step back, embarrassed and scared.

"Is Trevor here?" she asked her eyes curious and cautious.

"Yes, he is in his room."

"Would it be okay if I said hi? I have something for him." She smiled enthusiastically.

"Sure..." he said intrigued. He led her upstairs and down the hallway toward the last door on the left. He knocked twice, awkwardly waiting in silence for Trevor to answer the door. The vanilla and strawberry aroma began to fill his lungs again and he tried hard not to lean into her. Heat began to creep up his back onto his arms, making him roll up his plaid shirt higher. He heard her sharp intake of air when he did. He knew if he turned to look at her now he would have lost it right then. Images of him pushing her up against the wall kissing her luscious lips invaded his mind. He coughed hoping that would somehow clear it. He knocked on the door again, this time a little louder, praying that Trevor would answer the door. Sure enough, right after Andrew knocked for the second time, Trevor opened the door immediately, as if Trevor was on the other side of the door just standing there the whole time. He got a big smile on his face once he saw Eleanor.

"Hi, Trevor, I brought these for you. I hope you like chocolate?" she said, hopeful as she reached in her bag, pulling out a small white box they sold at the floral shop. Trevor's eyes beamed with excitement as he took the box and quickly opened it, surveying the variety of choices.

"These are double chocolate truffle...Oh, and these are chocolate covered cherries. I saved the best for last, my absolute favorite and I hope you like them too-they're chocolate covered bacon bites," she exclaimed, pointing to the chocolate bits in the box. Trevor automatically reached for those, shoving one in his mouth, carefully tasting each one. Once he was done with it, he grabbed another. He nodded enthusiastically, smiling brightly, as he tossed the box on his desk and wrapped Eleanor in a hug. She giggled as he pulled away.

Andrew was taken aback by the outburst, in awe of the chemistry they had together. He leaned back on

Trevor's door watching them interact. He truly admired that she took such liking to his brother. Maybe that was what Trevor needed, hell maybe that was what they both needed.

"Are you ready?" She asked, interrupting his thoughts again.

"Oh...yeah, follow me. They're out back in my shed," he replied, as she followed him out back. They walked in silence, the air thickened around them, electric-- as just before a thunderstorm.

He opened the shed and he heard her gasp, "Is this all of your mother's things?"

Andrew grimaced. He knew he should have cleaned up a little before she got here. There were boxes scattered everywhere and his work bench was covered with pictures and letters of his mothers. He watched her as she walked, in looking around at the chaos, picking up a picture that was lying on the bench. She studied it with a smile spreading across her face. Andrew relayed all the findings he found so far between his mom and her grandmother. He could see her relax more as they dug into each box looking for more clues.

"This is the postcard I found in my grandma's chest from your mother. I think Claire wanted me to see it, wanted to come here," she said quietly, trailing off.

"Why did you leave your home?" Andrew asked. He wasn't prepared when she gazed at him. A tormented expression crossed her face, her face worn and tired, the darkness under her eyes showing.

"I don't really want to talk about it...sorry," she muttered quietly, turning her head back down and looking at more pictures.

"Don't be..." Andrew stated, making Eleanor look at him again.

"I'm glad I am here." She weakly smiled, making all the air escape from his lungs.

"I am too..." he stated boldly smiling back at her. Her smile grew as her face became a deeper shade. All his bones in his body melted and fused themselves to one another.

"Would you like to stay for supper?" he blurted out in one breath.

"Um..." She glanced at him with uncertainty. "Sure?" she said, more as a question than an answer but Andrew took it as a yes.

"Andrew? Andrew, are you down there?" Becca's voice called from the balcony.

He sighed, his shoulders drooping, "Be right there!" he shouted, as he never breaking eye contact with Eleanor. Her face seemed to mimic his body actions.

"I guess maybe some other time then." She smiled, setting the picture down slowly, walking out the door. Not turning to look back at him as he hoped she would do.

CHAPTER SIX

"I am so glad you are here! It's been a rush since nine thirty this morning!" Rachel shouted to Eleanor, as she grabbed a group of roses cutting off the thorns. "Could you help Benjamin in the green house right now? He is the only one out there and it's pretty busy," she asked, looking frazzled.

"Sure!" Eleanor exclaimed, as she quickly punched into the time clock. She immediately grabbed her apron and headed to one of the three local greenhouses they had on site. After working at the store for a couple of weeks she had become less tense around Benjamin. She always kept her guard up though. She wasn't quite sure how to let it fully down, even if she tried.

Eleanor was happy today would be busy so she wouldn't have time to think about her time with Andrew two nights ago. She hardly got any sleep. Tossing and turning, hearing his deep husky voice echo through her head. She tried to put music on to drain it out, but it was no use. "Hello Elle, what pleasure do I owe to have you with me this beautiful afternoon?" Benjamin chuckled, as he continued to work on the flowers.

"Rachel wanted me to help you out here for an hour or two, hope you don't mind?" she asked, grabbing a hose, watering the hanging pots above.

"Oh, that would be great!" he said, grabbing the clippers and continuing to prune. They worked like that for quite some time not talking to each other. They were either attending to the customers or helping out the other employees with unloading trucks of sod and other materials. Occasionally they would glance at one another, Benjamin giving her his boyish smirk, making her mouth go dry.

"Hey Elle, can I ask you something?" Ben asked as he walked toward her, hanging up his apron behind the register. Her breath quickened, becoming nervous. "Sure,

what's up?" she asked, turning toward him.

"Would you like to go out to dinner with me this Friday?" he asked nervously, putting his hands in his pockets.

"Like a date?" she asked mystified.

"Well...actually, yeah!" he said very decidedly, making her look up, noticing the hopeful look on his face, smiling as he always did with his boyish grin.

She knew moving here would give her a lot of new opportunities, but also a lot of new battles. This one however, wasn't one she could win yet. Even though she had become more open and relaxed with him, being on a date or even in a relationship was foreign and scary as hell. "Um...I don't think that would be a good idea," she replied, frowning.

"Why not?" he asked crushed. Her shoulders slumped.

The last thing she wanted to do was hurt him.

"It's nothing against you Ben, I just," she started to say.

"No, it's okay, Elle. I know you haven't been here that long. What if I got a group together to head to the bar or something? Would you go then?" he asked, interrupting her, a hopeful smile spreading a crossed his face once more.

"Sure...who would be all there?" she asked, hoping that for sure Rachel would go. They have started to become good friends.

"It would be people from work mostly," he replied, reaching for the watering can on the shelf, setting it down next to the hose to fill it up.

She took a deep breath to calm her nerves. What harm would come from hanging out with a few friends? She knew she needed this, wanted this, nothing more than to defeat the fears and overcome her past. "I would love that." She smiled half-heartedly.

They didn't say much to each other for the rest of the night as they really didn't have much time.

Dusk approached and everyone grabbed their things to leave. Eleanor grabbed her purse and jacket, making her slow approach home, enjoying the peace and serenity that Hope Harbor had to offer. The sky was painted with yellow, soft purple, blue, and orange. In the far distance, bands were playing outside in the backyard of a bar, the soft sounds of the waves rolling onto the shore and the faint smell of sea salt mixed with the flowers from the store. It was moments like this she knew that she truly belonged here. She hadn't felt so much tranquility in a long time. "This is now and forever my home," she thought with a smile.

"I don't know if I can do this..." she thought to herself frantically searching through her closet for something decent to wear. "Maybe I should just stay home." She sighed, knowing too well she would regret it if she didn't go. Eleanor glanced at the bedroom clock for the fifth time, hoping the hand would move faster. She ran through the line of clothes hanging through the closet. She hopelessly decided on dark blue faded jeans and a floral blouse that bunched in front. Eleanor paced back and forth in her living room, waiting for Benjamin as her mind started to drift toward Andrew with his blue eyes. It made Eleanor weak in the knees. Whenever he talked, she was captivated by his deep, rich, husky voice, smooth as chocolate. She couldn't understand how she could be so attracted to a man that can't even touch her without her freaking out. She knew if someone looked up the phrase "messed up," they would see a picture of her right on the page. She couldn't honestly think of the last time she had been this attracted to someone other than a celebrity. This was different, foreign, and it scared her to the core.

Benjamin pulled up into the drive, making her come back to reality. "Wow, you look stunning!" he said, as he put the car in reverse and headed toward town.

She laughed nervously, "Thank you. You don't look too bad yourself." She turned to him to see him blush from the side of his face.

They headed to the local pub, Out on the Dock's, and parked on the side of the street opposite from it. She was surprised for a Saturday night that it was pretty quiet, but relieved that there wasn't a crowd. They headed inside finding their work group in the corner sitting in a large booth. The bar had a warm atmosphere. The walls were wooden panel and the countertops had small tea candles spaced a couple of feet apart giving a soft glow. There was a pool table off in the corner along with a dart board machine. The seats had red vinyl upholstery that formed to you when you sat. She could see Rachel laughing at a conversation and her eyes lit up when she saw them walk toward the table. Everyone greeted each other and Rachel scooted over so Eleanor could sit next to her, with Benjamin sitting next to Eleanor.

"What would you like to drink Elle? My treat?!" Benjamin said, as he handed her a menu. She looked through the selections, but settled on a nice, cold beer.

"Wouldn't peg you as a beer drinker, but I like your choice," he said as he got up from the booth, than headed to the bar.

"I am so glad you're here tonight Elle, this is the first time we have to hangout outside of work. That and now I don't have to worry about dealing with Benjamin's terrible cousin alone," she said smiling, squeezing Eleanor's arm.

Eleanor raised an eyebrow, "Who is Benjamin's cousin?"

"Becca, she is Andrew's girlfriend. Ugh, she is so materialistic. I don't know what Andrew sees in her. Of course, he probably only sees that she is drop dead gorgeous." Rachel said groaning as she turned out into the crowd. Eleanor followed Rachel's eyes to see a tall blonde, wearing a short black dress and long, lean legs. She looked as if she stepped out of the Victoria's Secret catalog.

"Is that Becca?" Eleanor asked, even though she was pretty sure she already knew the answer.

"Unfortunately..."Rachel sighed.

"You weren't kidding," she whispered, as her heart

sank lower into her chest.

Andrew scowled as he walked across the street to the pub that Becca's cousin Benjamin invited them to. Not that he was upset at her, but more upset at himself. He couldn't stop thinking about Eleanor. Ever since Becca saw Eleanor leave Andrew's shed that day, she would bring up Eleanor at every turn. He didn't know what Becca was thinking, but he wasn't going to ruin his chances with their relationship over Eleanor.

They walked into the bar and Becca started looking for Benjamin. "Hey, look! They are right over there." She stated as she took Andrew's hand and led him toward the table. His mouth opened in surprise when he smelled the vanilla and strawberry aroma. He glanced over and notices Eleanor sitting between Rachel and Benjamin, smiling at whatever they were talking about. Then he noticed Benjamin leaning in talking to Eleanor. How could she be so calm and collected with Benjamin and not to him? He had to get to the bottom of it.

"Hello Eleanor...." Andrew said quietly, making her look at him with her big autumn harvest eyes, sparkling like glass from the candle light. Every particle in his body melted and he began to sweat. She was intoxicatingly delectable and the atmosphere around him became electric.

"Hi." She smiled, slightly blushing before turning away. Becca grabbed the booth across from them and yanked Andrew to sit down next to her. An uncomfortable silence filled the table. Andrew noticed Eleanor try and sink into the cushion. He was baffled by the fact that she never fully seemed comfortable in her own skin.

"Ouch!" he hissed, feeling a sharp kick in his calf. He glared at Becca who batted her eye lashes innocently.

She patted his arm, giving him a sexy smirk. Under the table, she laid her hand on top of his inner thigh, stroking it with her thumb getting him aroused. He quickly grabbed her hand from his lap and held it with his, intertwining their fingers. Her smile grew wider and he couldn't help but smile back at her. Times like this made Becca irresistible to him.

"I'm Becca, by the way... Andrew's fiancée, you must be Eleanor." Becca smirked reaching her left hand across the table to shake Eleanor's, showing off her engagement ring. Andrew held his breath. He hadn't told Eleanor he was engaged. Eleanor's eyes quickly darted to Andrew then Becca, then back at Andrew. She smiled widely, gasping at the ring. "Congratulations!" She smiled brightly at Becca. "Your ring is beautiful!"

Benjamin began to discuss wedding details with Becca. Eleanor seemed intrigued with their conversation, but when she smiled at him it didn't reach her eyes. He knew he was the reason.

"Eleanor, may I get your next glass?" he asked, getting up from the booth.

"Um-yeah sure, thank you," she said, looking perplexed at him. Heat rose to her cheeks making them a beautiful shade of pink. He couldn't help but admire her beauty when she blushed. It made all those hard lines and frowns she usually had disappear.

"No problem," he said giving her a quick smile. "Becca, a mojito for you?" he said, turning to her seeing her mouth open, then close. Her eyes furrowed and her mouth scrunched up.

She turned to look at Eleanor then back at him. "No, I will have a beer as well." She said defiantly.

He raised an eyebrow confused because he knew that she hated beer. He hoped he hadn't made anything obvious about his feelings for Eleanor. He was positive that once he and Becca were married those feelings for Eleanor would vanish. "Women." he muttered to himself as he walked to the bar.

Everyone dispersed throughout the night, some played pool and darts while others were getting hammered at the bar. Becca, of course, was on the small dance floor by the jukebox with some other women. He wondered where Eleanor was as he scanned through the bar. He stopped and smiled when he noticed her alone by thewindow overlooking the water. He slowly walked up to her, "Hi."

She jumped back, spilling her beer all over her. Andrew reached for the napkins at the closest table. "Sorry! I didn't mean to scare you," he said apologetically, handing her the napkins.

As she wiped off her clothes; his mouth became dry when he noticed just how curvy her body appeared beneath her clothes. It sent waves of heat throughout his whole body. He turned away to look out the window, praying she didn't notice.

"It's okay," she replied, throwing the napkins away.

"How are you tonight?" he asked, hoping to strike up a conversation with her.

"I am fine, just not used to gatherings. I feel out of place." She sighed.

"It seems you're like that a lot," he said, turning back toward her.

"Well, I'm new here and don't know anyone. I'm still getting used to my surroundings," she replied, with a little harshness in her voice.

"Eleanor, I'm not trying to sound rude, but you know the people from work and you know me," he paused. "Well, more Trevor then me."

"It's nothing against you, Trevor just understands me," she stated honestly, with a sad gaze in her eyes.

"Well, I could understand you more if you let me," he grumbled, turning his head toward her. She didn't say anything but turned back away and gazed out the window, while biting on her lip, not being able to find the words.

"I am the plague to you, aren't I? Every time I am around you, it's like I'm a monster that you can't wait to get away from," he snapped.

"That's not fair, Andrew; don't make me feel guilty...I'm like that with everyone," she said angrily still not meeting his gaze. Fury ran through his veins. She was opening up to him, but not the way he intended her to.

"No, I'm pretty sure it's just me," he replied sarcastically. His eyebrows furrowed as he glared at her. She looked at him with anger in her eyes this time, her mouth formed into a hard line.

"Excuse me?" Her voice rose as her eyes widened and her breathing became ragged.

"I've been observing you with others. You seem to be fine with Benjamin and Trevor. It's just me. I don't get it, Eleanor. I have been racking my brain as to why you are so afraid of me. What happened Eleanor? I just don't get you!" he exclaimed, begging with his eyes for her to open up to him.

"Stop!" she cried, holding her hand up, stepping away from him once more. He noticed she started to shrink trying to disappear. "I don't want to talk about it," she huffed, trying to hold back her tears. "Why?" she paused. "Why do you even care?"

Her sadness struck his body like a lightning bolt. He could feel her sorrow and torment filled the air. It made his chest heavy, making it hard to breathe.

"I like you Eleanor, and I want to help you," he begged. "I want you to help but it's not that easy," she whispered as Andrew placed his hand on her arm to console her. His hand landed on her soft skin and a jolt of electricity shot thought him like a freight train. He looked down to see her shirt ruffled by the sleeve, bringing it up to her elbow. Andrew was alarmed, noticing a multitude of cigarette burns scattered on her arm. He thought pausing, "Elle...what are those?" he asked, gasping. Eleanor turned and looked down noticing what he was looking at. She pulled her arm away quickly, panic set in her eyes.

"Eleanor..." he responded but stopped when she shook her head, more tears rolling down her face. He dropped his hand to his side. She sniffled then quickly walked away. He watched her run into the bathroom. Rachel caught a glance of Eleanor. She turned back to Andrew glaring at him, and then quickly ran after Eleanor.

Andrew groaned turning his gaze back out the window. He hung his head as his heart felt too heavy for his chest. Andrew could only imagine the extent of what Eleanor was hiding. His chest ached just thinking if that was on her arm, just what else was hidden on her body. Was she harboring any worse scars than that?

"Eleanor, you okay?" Rachel asked her from the other side of the bathroom stall. Eleanor sunk to the floor trying to control her crying.

"Yea, I will be. Sorry, I hope I didn't ruin your night." Eleanor sniffed, trying to slow down her breathing.

"Oh honey you didn't; I am more worried about you. I saw you talking to Andrew. What happened?" Rachel asked as she sunk to the floor on the other side of the stall, reaching her hand under, to give Eleanor a tissue.

Eleanor's mind raced. She couldn't think straight and there was no way she could deal with letting anyone else in her heart at that time. "It was just a misunderstanding."

Rachel was quiet for a moment. Eleanor hoped she didn't hurt Rachel's feelings. "Honey, I know we don't really know each other. To tell you the truth, I just moved back here after college and sadly most of my friends have left. I haven't really made any new friends. The first moment we met I knew we would have a connection. I can tell you're dealing with a lot but I just want to let you know that I will be here for you. It's just- you remind me a lot of someone I used to know back at college." She said in a low voice. Eleanor's heart went out to her. She knew she wasn't the only one in the world that had demons and maybe Rachel had her own. Without another word, Eleanor got up, brushed herself off and opened the door. Rachel, still sitting on the ground looked up at Eleanor sadly. Eleanor reached out her hand and helped Rachel up, pulling Rachel into a tight hug. Neither one said anything to each other. Silence filled the bathroom and it was the sweetest melody that Eleanor ever heard.

"What is with you tonight?" Becca asked annoyed.

He sighed, reaching over to take her hands into his, "Nothing, I'm sorry. I just have a lot on my mind. I promise I will be better from now on."

She smiled, "I know you will love, because we have a lot to talk about with the wedding. Here I already made a list..." She trailed off digging into her Coach purse and pulling out a little black note book. Andrew did his best not to groan; wedding planning wasn't really on his list. He didn't want to think of his happiness when he could only imagine what pain Eleanor was going through. Maybe this was what he needed to be distracted by. Since she wouldn't let him in, there wasn't anything he could do for her. He smiled at Becca, squeezing her right hand, "Now let's see that list."

Andrew woke up before dawn and headed down to the dock where he liked to think. He left Becca sleeping peacefully in his warm bed, as he braved the chill of the morning air. He actually didn't mind it since he spent most of his days out on a boat anyway. Once again he couldn't sleep because his dreams were plagued by Eleanor's voice. Always the same dream over and over again.

He headed for a bench on the tail end of the dock, sitting while he watched the sun begin to peek over the water's horizon. The sky cascaded with rich oranges and yellows, turning the darkness of the ocean to turquoise as the colors danced on the water's crest. He did his best last night to try and be excited about the wedding, but trying to get excited over colors and wedding cake flavors didn't really amuse him. He was actually surprised that Becca was taking this wedding full on; they even set a date last night. Two months from now they would be saying their- I do's at the nearest botanical garden. He wasn't quite sure what the rush was and when he asked, she was hesitant to answer. Her enthusiasm seemed like an act.

"I just want to be married to you, sweetheart; I have been dreaming about this day forever." She smiled brightly at him, but Andrew noticed it didn't reach her eyes.

He knew there was more than she was letting on with the wedding and he was determined to find out, he just didn't know how. But until then he had to stay away from Eleanor; she was just consuming his mind and he hadn't been able to think clearly. With his feelings unfolding, he wouldn't let these thoughts jeopardize his relationship with Becca and their engagement. He wondered if he would be able to have the strength to stay away.

CHAPTER SEVEN

A month after the bar scene, Eleanor still did her best not to dwell on her conversation with Andrew. She hadn't seen him since and she could only think that she scared him away. She used her free time to hang out with Rachel on shopping sprees, girls's nights, and fixing up her new home.

"What are you in the mood for tonight?" Rachel asked as she lounged on Eleanor's couch as Eleanor put away her groceries.

"Girls night in, we could do dinner and a movie?" Eleanor asked. Rachel scratched her head as she turned over on the couch but instead fell off it. Both women roared, laughing contagiously. "You, my friend, are clumsy. You're cut off, no wine for you!" Eleanor laughed. She sighed, she was so happy to find a friend like Rachel. In a way her personality matched that of Claire's. She couldn't help but smile to herself.

"But... but...I'm the one who bought the wine." Rachel pouted doing her best puppy eyes impression.

Eleanor laughed. "Okay...fine, but that face won't win me all the time."

"Hey, that could have earned me an Oscar right there. I should start acting. I think I am a natural," she exclaimed, tossing her head back, arching her back and putting her hand through her hair as if she were on a photo shoot. Eleanor grabbed the pillow from the side chair and threw it at her, laughing. She noticed she laughed a lot around Rachel. It helped her forget her pain and a certain someone's brooding eyes. Except when she would mention him, which tended to be a lot more often the past couple weeks.

"Can you believe Andrew and Becca are getting married next month? Talk about a short engagement! What is the rush?" Rachel asked, walking into the kitchen and grabbing a bag of chips.

"I have no idea..." Eleanor mumbled.

"You know he hasn't come in the flower shop for the past couple weeks. Ever since that night at the bar...I wonder why," she thought to herself. Eleanor didn't want to think about him. She was more worried about Trevor. She constantly wondered how he was taking it and she missed their talks. "All I know is that Becca sure didn't like you," Rachel chuckled.

Eleanor was surprised, "Why would you say that?"

"That night she made a point of showing off her ring to you. She ordered a beer because you did. Then when you and Andrew were talking she had a death stare at you. She was trying to use the force on you. Dude, she was totally jealous." Rachel snorted a laugh as she opened a bag of chips and started to munch. Eleanor grabbed the bag out of her hand putting it on the counter. She stood in front of her friend with her hands on her hips.

"That is insane. I know he doesn't even have feelings for me like that," she stated, exhausting herself by the mere fact of stating it out loud, and her heart seemed to sink a little. No one had ever felt that way toward her. She wouldn't even know what to feel or how to react if they did. Rachel frowned. "Don't talk about yourself like that hun. Matter of fact, I see the way he stares at you sometimes, and I highly doubt that he just likes you only as a friend."

"Sad thing is, even if he did...I would never know. It's too late." Eleanor cried, slumping onto the couch.

It seemed pretty steady for a Wednesday with a bunch of tourists coming into the shop to survey at the chocolates. Eleanor had been bouncing between departments, helping whoever she could during the rushes. They were running out of arrangements, especially her newest designs, three big bright yellow tulips with a variety of red and white roses mixed in with baby's breath and pink small carnations. She made about ten of them and by midafternoon they only had three left.

Eleanor heard somebody walk up to the counter and cough. She turned around to be appalled at the sight of the man standing in front of her. The last person she ever thought to see here, her uncle Ron. Her veins burned with rage and her heart began to pound.

"What are you doing here?" she asked bluntly.

"Oh...I was just in the neighborhood...and I thought I would stop in and say hi," he said with a smirk on his face, giving her a smart ass expression.

"How did you find me?" she asked furiously, the last thing she ever wanted was to see him.

"Oh darling...I have my ways," he said winking at her, amused at her mood. "See the thing is...you have something that is mine and I would like it back."

She dropped the scissors she was holding, afraid that she would like to use it on him. How dare he come here after what he put her through?

"I have nothing that is yours! Haven't I given you enough as it is?" she snarled at him.

"You haven't given me anything! That money was supposed to be mine in the first place, but no....you had to walk in and ruin everything!! You and that wretched mother! I want my money!" he snapped back, the veins in his forehead protruding. His face looked like a lobster and she wouldn't be surprised to see steam blowing out his ears. "Your life has been perfect. Claire gave you everything you ever wanted and left the rest of us with nothing!" he shouted, slamming his fist on the table. Luckily most of the guests didn't hear it.

That struck a nerve, and it took everything she had to resist punching him, "Perfect?!...What is so perfect when your own mother stops loving you? Leaving you alone for days on end going hungry and having to fend for yourself? Even better how about when your home, you get beaten by your mom's drug dealing boyfriend. Then one day she decides she doesn't want you anymore and just drops you off on the steps without saying goodbye. I know you never liked me because of my mother; you all thought I was going to become her but guess what? I will never be her!! How dare you even say that about your own mother? I will not have you stand here and disrespect her or myself. Leave! Or I will call the police!" she shouted. Eleanor was furious, close to tears, but she would never let him see her cry; not in a million years.

"You have no right to speak to me..." he started shouting, when a voice that Eleanor knew too well cut him off.

"I think she told you to leave, now leave...or I will make you!" Andrew growled his voice like thunder, standing a foot taller than her uncle. Ron turned around to see Andrew flexing his muscles, standing there like a mountain. Andrew's jaw clenched, eyes furrowed as he looked at Ron. He raised his hand, backing up and turning when he got to the door. He glanced behind his shoulder at her, glaring at her like a vulture before a kill.

He opened the door, but stopped to scowl at her, "This isn't over yet!" he shouted slamming the door shut. She exhaled sharply, not realizing that she had been holding her breath. Eleanor's whole body shook from fury and tears slowly rolled down her cheeks. She looked up at Andrew, who was staring at her with concern in his eyes.

"Go take a breather, Eleanor," he said calmly as his copper, brown five o'clock shadow made his eyes dazzle.

"Yes, go…I can watch it from here," Rachel said with a somber tone as she rubbed Eleanor's back, letting her know that she saw the whole thing. Eleanor exhaled and nodded, looking down at the floor, afraid that if she met their eyes she would start to cry. She headed outside to the back of the store where there was a bench under an old maple tree. She placed her head into her hands, staring at the ground. She took a few deep breaths trying to breathe in the calming smell of the flowers around her. Instead she kept seeing flashes of her uncle's face and all the ill memories of him and his sister while she was growing up. She couldn't understand why he had to show up when she was finally getting her life back together.

Suddenly, a pair of boots came into her view standing right in front of her. "I thought you might like a glass of water." Andrew said, sitting down next to her. She sat up taking the glass of water, keeping her eyes straight ahead. The smell of his musk filled her lungs and made her body hum. She wanted to scoot away towards him but she couldn't.

The bench was too small. Their knees touched each other's and she couldn't help but feel an electric current run through her. She wondered if he felt it too.

"Thank you." she sighed, sipping the cold water

slowly. "You know I had it taken care of, you didn't need to come in and rescue me. I'm not that kind of girl."

He groaned, "Eleanor, I realized that. I was just trying to help."

Her head jerked up, her eyes piercing through him, "No, you think I'm just some damsel in distress. I am stronger than you think."

Andrew raised his hand up toward her, as to touch her shoulder. "I am not here to fight with you. I know you're still mad about the other night. I came here to apologize."

"What to make it up to me before you get married?" she shouted, turning away, adrenaline pulsating through her body. She needed to relax before she said something she would regret. She sighed. "I'm sorry. I just thought when I moved here, my past wouldn't follow me..." Hanging her head, she focused on the glass in her hand and the way the water swirled in it, trying to calm herself.

"All those things you said about growing up... and your mother..." he said, trailing off, as his eyes studied her facial expressions. "Were they true?" he asked, not answering her previous question.

"Yes..." she whispered, as flashbacks slammed into her hiding under her bed, breathing as lightly as she could so he wouldn't find her. Unfortunately, he always knew where she was and would drag her out by her hair. She flinched, coming back to the present, but remembering the horrendous pain of him punching, kicking, and burning her.

"Do you have these all over your body?" he asked sadly.

She didn't look at him right away.

"Oh God, I am so sorry. No one deserves this," he

sympathized, touching her arm as she rolled the sleeves back down. He sent a pulse of electricity up through her arm again, shooting into her whole body, making her jump. "Sorry," he apologized, but didn't remove his hand. It felt warm, heating her blood like afire.

"You can't erase the past, but I've learned that it's not good to hide behind it either. Sad thing is that my uncle is right. He isn't going to leave without a fight. I don't know what he has up his sleeve, but I know it won't be good." She groaned and leaned back on the bench, staring up at the sky.

Eleanor glanced at Andrew's clenched hands, his veins protruding from his muscular arms. He had his face turned away from her but she could tell he was angry; she could feel the air change. It was a strong magnetic charge it, felt as if she were standing out in a thunderstorm. He turned to her with his hands still in fists and his eyes set ablaze, blue swirled with specks of bright golden hue.

"He won't do anything while I am around. He won't stand a chance with me. If you have any problems, just call me." He nodded reassuring her as well as himself. "Promise me you will," he said pleading, bringing his hand back up toward her neck. She nodded but then froze. Images raced through her head of Dan, grabbing her by the throat and slamming her against the wall, when she took a dollar out of her mom's purse. It was when she wasn't allowed to go to her grandma's and her mother didn't leave any food, leaving Eleanor to starve.

She shook her head to clear her thoughts and continued to look at him. He didn't take his eyes off her; his eyes were steady and surprisingly calmed her. He lightly grabbed the ring that was around her neck.

"Was this your grandmas?"

"Yes, this was her engagement ring," she stated.

"It's beautiful," he said quietly. In his eyes she could tell that his mind was turning. She didn't want to ask though, she didn't think she could handle much more of today.

He coughed. "I am still willing to have you help me look for information about your grandmother and my mom if you're still interested. I have more free time on my hands now," he said nonchalantly making her curious at what he meant by those last words.

She gave him a puzzled look, "Yeah, I would like that." His shoulders seemed to relax and he exhaled as if a weight had been lifted.

"So umm..." he coughed, "You and Benjamin... how is that going?" he said casually looking down when he asked but then back up at her while his fingers folded together.

"Um-it's not going." she replied raising an eyebrow in confusion. "He asked me out but I said no. I am not looking to date anyone just yet. I don't think I would be able to if I tried. Yes, I'm talking to you right now which is a big feat for me, but I've come to the conclusion the more I know and spend time with someone, the less my wall stacks up around me. Since you know my secret, I have a strange sense that I can trust you. It scares the crap out of me though," Eleanor said, glancing tentatively at him. "I hate feeling vulnerable and exposed. My secret, I felt, was the only thing that could make me strong, but it was also my weakness." She paused, sensing she was rambling. "However, getting back on the subject, I don't think I am the one Benjamin really wants to date," she commented flatly, wishing secretly that Andrew was the one she was going on a date with. She looked at Andrew who opened his mouth to speak but then closed it. He even appeared to be blushing, which was a beautiful sight to see.

"Oh, well, I highly doubt there could be anyone else. I mean you..."he said, stopping himself. "So you don't like him then?"

She blushed, looking back at the ground kicking her feet in the dirt, "Yes and no." she whispered.

She saw him look at her out of the corner of her eye. "Yes and no?" he asked confused.

She turned to him blushing again and sighed, "It's complicated." He nodded, accepting her answer as he gazed out over the garden. "How about you and Becca...how are the wedding plans coming along?" she asked nervously.

"They're not...I broke off the engagement with her." He told her truthfully, sighing as his shoulders sagged and he rested his arms on his knees, fiddling his thumbs together. She felt sorry for him- something serious must have happened for him to break it off with her. They were the couple of the town.

"I'm sorry Andrew. I knew something was up with you that morning on the dock. I didn't want to push you about it though. May I ask what happened?" she asked, resting her hand on his shoulder, feeling his muscle under her hand twitch.

He looked up and for a second she could see pain in his eyes, but just as fast as it appeared it was gone. He then gave her a half-hearted smile. "It's complicated..."

Eleanor grimaced and her heart dropped a little for him. "I understand. I am sorry for whatever made your relationship end. For whatever it was, it's her loss. I would make sure not to screw up something so good." she declared honestly, blushing at the fact that she confessed something about her feelings toward him.

Talking with him, expressing her feelings, emotions, and secrets made her wall crumble a little more and actually boosted her confidence. She never really had a man she could actually converse with and she had to admit it felt pretty damn good.

With those words, Andrew sat up straight, an unforeseen passion in his eyes as he leaned toward her. He tucked a strand of hair behind her ear, leaving his hand there, caressing her cheek with his thumb. Her hormones went into a fury. Her brain once again interrupted her mind, "Run, Eleanor, run!" Her heart begged her to stay. Eleanor knew she wanted to stay, she oddly felt safe with his soft touch.

"Oh...Eleanor," he sighed heavily, his face inches from hers. She was frozen, mesmerized by his luscious lips, so inviting. She was startled when she looked into his eyes for she had never seen such desire illuminate from someone. It surrounded them. A thick fog of sexual tension and electricity rose between them. Her urge for him to take her right then and there was so powerful her thighs began to ache. Her brain shouted, "Stop, Eleanor, he will hurt you!" Before she knew it, she stood up brushing off her clothes as if she were trying to shake the fog away. She breathed a sigh in defeat, the sensation of ecstasy lifted from her chest, leaving by a dull uneasiness.

"I think I should be getting back inside, they are probably wondering where I am." She breathed in a rush, turning and walking back inside without looking back, afraid to see the look on his face.

Andrew knew that he should have just left right then and there. His heart had been played with enough times in the past week. What just happened between him and Eleanor wasn't helping the healing process. Starting from the night he broke up with Becca, which was, ironically, the same night he met Eleanor and her friends at the bar. Becca came home with Andrew and things began to get hot and heavy. Both were sweating, panting, and craving each other desperately. Becca kneeled in front of Andrew as she undid the back of her lacy pink bra, throwing it seductively on the floor as she locked her eyes with his. Andrew's erection grew to the point he had to unzip his pants to let it free. Becca lunged forward as her lips devoured his. Her kisses were slow then fast making Andrew grow more impatient. He knew if he didn't have her soon that he would combust. He grabbed Becca around the waist with one hand, flipping her over to her back, as she let out a seductive giggle. He groaned at the sight of her light skin glowing from the fireplace and her perky breasts arousing him further. He took one in his mouth, making her moan loudly. He quickly reached down to the matching panties, yanking them off in one swift motion. He reached over to the night stand, grabbing a condom and rolling it on. As he slowly entered her, he saw her eyes roll back as she smiled in pure ecstasy. He leaned his head back and his erection filled her. He thought of nothing but how her warm soft curves fit into his hard physique. His mind suddenly clicked to the time where he noticed just how intoxicatingly delicious Eleanor's curves were. With that thought in his head, he moaned, "Eleanor…"

Becca's body went stiff, making Andrew's mind come back to the present. "Excuse me? Did you just say, Eleanor?"

He groaned as his stomach did a flip, thinking. "Did I really just say that out loud?"

She pushed him off of her and covered herself with

the blanket. "Are you cheating on me with her?" she cried.

"No! Of course not, Trevor mentioned that he wanted to go to the floral shop and I figured it was because of Eleanor...so I guess her name just popped in my head." he lied, his face becoming flushed. Luckily it was dark in the room so she couldn't tell.

She raised her eyes brows in disbelief. "So... you're not cheating on me?" she asked, hesitantly.

"No, I would never do that to you...I'm so sorry, love," he cooed, turning on his side to stroke her arm when she stopped him.

"Andrew-I've been cheating on you." she cried, turning away from him.

His body froze his blood raging in his veins. He blinked a couple times making sure this wasn't a dream.

"Is that why you wanted to rush our wedding?" he asked, trying to keep calm when in reality his brain was screaming. His muscle locked up and he felt like he was going to throw up right then and there.

She whimpered, "Yes. I love you Andrew, you know I do." She paused, looking down at the bed. "My dad set me up with this guy named Patrick. He thought it would be better for our family since he is socially ranked as I am. I just did this so my dad would lay off of me getting married to you. Things just happened to get a little carried away."

Andrew sat up in bed, his fist clenched, "You think? Did it ever occur to you how it would have turned out? Did you even think about my feelings? Your dad wanted this so he could get me out of the way...couldn't you see that or were you too busy with your tongue down the guy's throat?"

"Yes, I did, but I tried, Andrew, I really did," she

cried, as she cradled her head in her hands.

"Do you love him?" he asked as a wave of nausea overwhelmed him again. He took deep breaths to try to push it away. He couldn't believe this was happening. How could he have been this stupid? His head had been so wrapped up with Eleanor, the wedding, and his mother's past; he couldn't see the storm raging on right in front of him.

"Andrew-I" she cried harder.

"Answer the damn question!" Andrew shouted, getting out of bed as he tried to find his clothes in the dark, avoiding her gaze.

"I never meant to hurt you," she replied, wiping away her tears.

He knew that was a lie and a cover up. With that Andrew got up, put on his pants and shirt and headed for the door. "I'm heading to work, by the time I get back, you better be gone." He paused, as he tried to blink away the tears. "And keep the damn ring."

"Oh, Andrew!" she bawled, as he walked out of the room. He bounded down the steps in his back yard and headed for his truck. He got in and slammed the truck door. He banged his arms against the steering wheel. His rage got the best of him and much to his displeasure, he started to cry. He thought it could be the high from the sexual adrenaline or lack of sleep. His head slumped onto the steering wheel and he let himself have those few moments of weakness.

CHAPTER EIGHT

"You look like shit man, what happened?" Ryan asked, wiping his brow as he hauled equipment onto their old sturdy forty--five foot boat, Lucy. Andrew knew there was no way that he could not tell Ryan. He wouldn't be surprised if everyone in Hope Harbor already found out. That is what he got for living in a small community, he supposed. He had to ponder on what Eleanor might think about it. "Hello, Earth to Andrew?" Ryan asked, giving Andrew a light punch on the arm.

"Ugh, yea, Becca and I are done. She cheated on me, end of story," Andrew stated bluntly as he climbed on the ancient looking vessel. Paint chipped on the sides, rust on some of the metal, but the engine just got refurbished. She looked like hell but sounded and ran like a beaut.

"I'm sorry, Andrew. That is serious bullshit. I'm glad you found out now before you married her." Silence filled the air, which surprisingly calmed Andrew. The sound of waves hitting the boat with a soothing rhythm put Andrew in a better mood and he did his best to completely distract his mind with his work.

Once they reached their destination, Ryan slowed the hull a few knots as Andrew hooked the buoys, attaching the line to a pulley to help him pull a set of three traps out of the water. Once all three traps were laid out on the wooden railing of the boat, he and Ryan pulled out any lobsters they thought were potential keepers. First, they banded the claws together, pull out their double sided gauge and measured the carapace of the lobster. Then they throw the legal ones in the holding tank. Once all of the traps were hauled and cleaned, Ryan baited as Andrew drove the boat so they could drop the traps back down.

They did this every day, but Andrew couldn't be happier. He planned on lobstering for the rest of his life. It was funny that this was how Ryan and Andrew met. They knew each other in school but didn't really become friends until their junior year, when Andrew helped Ryan's dad on the boat, willing to learn everything he could about lobstering so he could help pay his mom's hospital bills.

Bringing the boat back up to the dock, he absent-mindedly was thinking of Becca who would be there to greet them as she did almost every day, generally complaining about the smell. But instead today he was greeted by someone else. The one person he couldn't stop thinking about, like she stepped right out of his dream: Eleanor. She was waiting on the dock with Trevor right next to her, smiling. Ryan peered back at him, smirking. Andrew wished fleetingly that this could be his sight every day for the rest of his life.

"Hello, Trevor!" A beautiful red--haired man smiled, walking toward them on the docks. Eleanor swore he could be a model if he wasn't so dirty from being out on the ocean. He had a smile that stretched for miles.

"You must be Eleanor. I've heard so much about

you. My name is Ryan." He grinned even brighter, showing off his shimmering, hazel eyes. He reached out his hand to shake hers. Eleanor panicked, but felt as if she needed to do this. She quickly shook his hand once then dropped it. Ryan smiled slightly, a perplexed look in his eyes, but let it go.

From a distance Eleanor saw Andrew getting off the boat, her breath catching. It was the first time she ever saw him in his garb. He looked breath-taking even with his face smeared with grease and his trousers were filled with things she didn't even want to think about. When the sun hit his face as he approached them, she could see he was tired.

"It's nice to meet you, Ryan. Trevor and I brought you both some cookies that we baked with Elizabeth." She smiled sweetly, reaching her hands out displaying the goodies.

"Aw man, I hope these are her famous chocolate blueberry cookies!" Ryan shouted excitedly, reaching out, grabbing a handful, and shoving two in his mouth. Eleanor could help but giggle at him. She noticed out of the corner out of her eye that Andrew never took his eyes off of her and how sad he looked. Every fiber in her body wanted to hug him, but her brain decided against it. Ryan broke her thoughts as he took the whole container, turning toward Trevor. They both walked back toward land, leaving her alone with Andrew.

Every hair on her body stood on end. She looked up at Andrew who was continuing to stare at her. "Everything okay?" she asked, worried.

He blinked, seeming like he was coming back from a trance. "What? -Oh, yeah. Sorry, I am just tired." he mumbled. Andrew ran his hand through his hair, letting out a big sigh.

"What brought you over today? I am glad Trevor got to see you. Did you guys have fun together?" Andrew asked, slinging his bag over his shoulder. They both started walking toward his truck.

"I saw Trevor playing outside and thought I would stop over and say hi. Elizabeth is a really lovely lady. You can tell that she adores him. He was so excited to make cookies for you both. Elizabeth told me many stories of you and Trevor growing up," Eleanor gabbed. She hated that she felt like she was just rambling on and on. She pulled her jacket a little tighter around her.

"They're going to town on those...I will be surprised if I get any," he chuckled quietly. Eleanor liked the sound of his laugh, it made the hard lines on his forehead disappear, even if it was only for a few seconds. He looked years younger. She could only hope that he would tell her what he is going through. She realized they weren't that close but he knew more about her than most people and she could only hope that he would open up to her.

"Here you can have mine. I already ate some at the house," she said, grabbing the bag of cookies out of her pocket, waiting for his hand to reach out. When he did, she dropped the bag of cookies in his hand, trying not to touch him. Andrew, quickly took the cookies but touched her hand lightly, taking his other hand and caressing the top of hers.

Eleanor's heart was going a mile a minute. She was scared, but she couldn't deny that warm sensation from his hand felt nice. She tried to pull away gently; at first he resisted but then reluctantly let go. She quickly put her hand into her pocket.

"Sorry," she said quietly. She had no reason to apologize. She wished she wasn't so afraid for him to touch her. It scared her initially but once she felt him there, it wasn't so bad.

"No, I am sorry. It hasn't been my day." Andrew frowned. "Thank you for the cookies," he added, putting the bag in his pocket. At that point they reached Ryan and Trevor. Ryan and Andrew began talking work, and Trevor busied himself chasing a butterfly. Eleanor didn't say much, but was very entertained watching Trevor. He had such an innocence about him. She wished that she could see what he saw. She knew he saw the world differently. It would be a nice break from her life right now. They headed toward the cars. Eleanor said goodbye to Ryan and Trevor, both hopping into the truck. She felt the tension between her and Andrew. It made the cool breeze from the water feel like a hot summer day. He turned toward her, darkness passing through his eyes, clouding the blue. "I will see you around Eleanor. Thank you for being with Trevor today. You're really good to him," he said sincerely.

"He is a good kid, but I'm not the only one that is good to him," she replied. "You do an amazing job with him. I don't think you get told that enough. Just because he is quiet and keeps to himself doesn't mean you're not getting through to him. I wanted to let you know that. I don't know what you're going through but Andrew..." She paused. "I will be here to listen. You have been there for me when I when I needed saving from myself. I thank you and want to return the favor." Eleanor reassured him.

Eleanor noticed Andrew's eyes grow soft. It crushed her to see him like this. Her shaking hand slowly touched his arm. He looked down at his arm, then back up at her. "Thank you, Eleanor, that is truly one of the sweetest things anyone has ever said to me. You have no idea how much your words have touched me. I will Eleanor. I am so glad you're here." Andrew whispered. Eleanor had such an urge to hug him, but her mind fought against it. She dropped her hand and nodded smiling sweetly. He nodded then got into the truck with the others. He looked out the window at Eleanor one more time. Her body burst at the warmness in his eyes. He smiled. She waved as he pulled out of the drive and she walked toward her car. She glanced out on the water and couldn't help but smile as she hugged herself, holding on to the heat she felt by him.

CHAPTER NINE

When Benjamin asked Eleanor to the gig at the bar on Friday she couldn't help but speculate whether it was a date or not. She was afraid to ask so she figured she would wait and see how the night went. However, she knew if the night turned out to be a date, she would have to decline once more. It wasn't that she didn't like him as more than a friend, but the whole idea of dating scared her.

Friday came faster than Eleanor expected. When they locked up for the night, Eleanor was torn between dread and excitement for the night's events. It had been a long week, especially after the incident with her uncle and Andrew. Since that day, her mind was continually drawn back to Andrew.

Eleanor secretly hoped that Andrew would make an appearance at the bar. But who was she kidding? She shouldn't be harboring the little feelings she had for Benjamin, but yet have this yearning for Andrew at the same time. She thought about maybe cancelling, but then she knew
it wouldn't be fair to Benjamin. These thoughts continued to nag her as she got home from work and also when she arrived at the bar. There was a chill in the air, making her pull her leather jacket a little tighter.

She loved the nighttime in Maine. Nature came

alive with hundreds of lightning bugs dancing with each other in the wind. The distant sounds of the waves crashing acted like drums of war. The moon, a silvery spotlight, displayed the beauty and talents of the earth. Sweet smells of the salty air mingled with honeysuckle. She couldn't help but feel butterflies swarm in her stomach. She liked Benjamin but her mind was becoming more bewitched with Andrew each passing day. She honestly didn't know what to think about Andrew and her. She knew he needed time to heal, and so did she from her tormented past.

Once there, she texted Benjamin telling him that she was outside. She heard the band warming up and doing vocal checks. Benjamin told her that they're a local band that played at Tuggar's often. She saw Benjamin come out of the front door and her jaw dropped, seeing him wearing tight faded jeans and a tight black shirt showing muscle that she didn't know he had.

"Hello, beautiful!" He smiled at her leaning in for a quick hug. It left a burning sensation over her body.

"Hi, you look very nice!" she smiled giving him a head to toe look. He gave her his boyish grin that made her knees go weak.

"Why thank you...you look stunning as always." He smiled, taking her hand as they wove through the crowd to get inside where they had their own booth reserved off the side of the stage. They sat down, looking at the stage as Benjamin snuggled up closer to her, putting his arm around her. She felt his skin on hers; the softness of his hand caressing her exposed shoulder, goose bumps running down her arm.

"What would you care to drink?" he asked, leaning in close and whispering in her ear. She could feel his hot breath on the nape of her neck. It was a sensation that made her temperature rise. She gulped loudly and without thinking leaned away. She looked at him from the corner of her eye. His eyes grew soft and a sweet smile flashed across his face. He met her gaze and nodded. He patted her hand softly. "It is okay, Elle."

She couldn't help but ponder at his expression and what his words meant. She nodded and said, "I would like some sweet red wine, if they have any?"

"Your wish is my command." He smiled back as he headed toward the bar. She was glad she felt comfortable with him because with Andrew, she would have combusted if he touched her that way.

As Eleanor waited for him to return she glanced around the building. The walls were a light grey, the woodwork a deep cherry chestnut brown that made the atmosphere warm and inviting. There was a multitude of various artwork and decorations hanging in harmony that reflected Hope Harbor perfectly. She leaned back into the booth snuggling up against the deep red cushions, sighing. She would have never thought in a million years that her life would ever end up this way.

"Life is filled with difficult situations and if you don't learn how to deal with them and overcome them, they will trap and consume you. You would never feel the breeze on your face, the warmth of sun heating your blood." Claire's words echoed through her mind. From this moment she was going to live by Claire's quotes. Starting tonight, Eleanor was going to embrace the future instead of focusing on the past. She needed it more than ever, she couldn't survive if she didn't.

"Here you go darling...I hope you like it." Benjamin smiled as he broke into her thoughts. He scooted into the booth handing her a wine glass. She smiled back as she took the glass, smelling it, an aroma of tantalizing cherry, blackberry, with a splash of strawberry that made her mouth water. It tasted as divine as it smelled. She slowly sipped the savory tonic, bringing a pleasant vibe to her body as she relaxed.

"Oh, by the way...Rachel is going to meet us up here," Benjamin stated, rushing out his words in one breath as to break the tension that was plaguing him.

Her mouth dropped, "Wait, so... this isn't a date?" she asked. She should have known better.

She could hear him sigh, "Elle...I'm sorry. I wasn't sure myself if it was a date since you rejected me the first time, which I totally understand. I just wanted to spend time with you alone, to see if we could maybe be something more." He blushed. "But I was telling her about the band and she wanted to come...what was I supposed to say?"

"No, it is okay," she trailed off, smiling at him.

"I will just say that I invited you too." He said, trying to reassure her. She felt stupid that she thought that this could have been a date. She took a big gulp of wine. Screw this, she was going to enjoy herself. Within the next ten minutes, she finished her wine. She headed to the bar for another, and when she got back to the table Benjamin gave her a surprised look, "What are you drinking?"

She smirked, "Whiskey sour."

She sat down without giving him another look, taking a drink of it. It was strong but smooth, going down easily.

They didn't say much after that as they both were too engaged with the band that started to play.

Shortly after, Rachel arrived looking stunning, wearing tight jeans with a black V-neck shirt. Out of the corner of her eye, she could see Benjamin's reaction, his mouth dropping. "Hello, Rachel, you look gorgeous, as usual!" Eleanor grinned at Rachel. No way could she be mad at her. She had no reason to be mad in the first place. She noticed that Rachel sure got dolled up tonight and wondered if it was for him.

She knew she would have to quiz her about it later "Eleanor! I didn't know you were going to be here." she said surprised taking the seat across from her.

"Benjamin asked me as we were walking out of work today about it and he told me you were going to be here so I had to come!" Eleanor exclaimed happily, taking her hand and squeezing it. She knew Benjamin would thank her later.

"Would you ladies like a drink? Elle, would you like another whiskey sour?" Benjamin asked, taking her empty glass. She didn't realize she finished it already. They both nodded and Benjamin scooted out of the booth and headed toward the bar. The band started to pick up and play an upbeat song that Eleanor couldn't help but dance. Rachel did the same.

Benjamin returned with their drinks. Benjamin returned with their drinks as Eleanor and Rachel took a break from dancing. He and Rachel began a conversation about the band and how Benjamin knew the drummer. Eleanor sat back listening to the conversation and studying their chemistry together. She shook her head because she should have seen this all along. They were made for each other, Rachel's eyes glowing vibrantly while Benjamin was talking and the way he looked at her as if she were a treasure he just found. She could feel this warm sensation around, as if their love for each other was wrapping them in a cocoon.

There was a crowd that was starting to form around the band when they started to play Journey's, *Separate*

Ways. Eleanor got excited because she hadn't heard that song in forever. She told Benjamin and Rachel they should go up by the band. They asked her to join them, but she didn't want to interrupt the magic that was unfolding between them. Instead Eleanor went up and got herself a third whiskey sour. Her body started to become all warm and tingly, she had never felt this way before and kind of liked it. Once she got back to the booth she could see Benjamin and Rachel in the crowd holding hands.

Eleanor searched in her purse to find her camera so she could take pictures of the band, but instead found Andrew's number. Her heart jumped just thinking of him and her stomach became flooded with butterflies. She bit her lip, thinking, "Should I text him?" She typed in the message box, "Hi Andrew, this is Eleanor, how are you?" She didn't send it to him right away. She contemplated for five minutes as she took a big gulp of her whiskey sour. It burned going down, making her cringe. She fumbled holding her phone and glass in the same hand. Her thumb slipped as it hit send. She gasped, thinking "Crap!"

She couldn't help but stare at her phone hoping and dreading for the reply text. Instantly she got a ping back from him, "Hey. I am doing well, your date not going good?"

Reading the text she became confused, "Who told you I was on a date?"

"A little birdie told me. So I guess it's not going well?" he replied

"Why would you say that? And no, it's not a date," she stated.

"Because your texting me. What do you mean it's not a date?" he wrote.

"Because that is what he told me. Rachel is here. I can obviously tell that they have a thing together. They would make a cute couple. I feel very stupid and fuzzy right now," she replied.

He didn't text back for a couple of minutes, making her nervous, wondering what he was thinking. The ping from her phone made her jump. Her mind was elsewhere. She quickly read it. "I'm sorry. It is his loss...Fuzzy? Have you been drinking?"

She took another big swig as she read his text. She didn't know what to send back. She really didn't want to tell him that she was pretty buzzed. She set the phone down as she got up for another drink before she got too caught up. This time she was really feeling the effects of the alcohol. Her head began to spin, bringing every beat of the song and melody to life and she couldn't help but sway to the music.

When she got back to the table, she read Andrew's text. "You know you have a lot to offer as well. Just haven't found the right person. Where are you? I'm coming to get you."

Eleanor was positive that he was just being nice to her because of the situation at hand. She couldn't think of anything she could offer anyone. She was damaged goods, past the expiration, worn and torn. He clearly didn't know what he was talking about, but that didn't stop her from wanting to be near him. She was like a fly heading toward a bug zapper that happened to be gorgeous as hell.

"I'm at Tuggar's," she responded, hiccupping into another glass of whiskey sour. At this point, she wanted to drink the last twenty-five years of her life away so she wouldn't be able to feel for once.

One glance at that message and Andrew grabbed his keys, hopping in his truck, speeding down to Tuggar's to get her. She was drunk and alone thanks to Benjamin not staying with her. Fury raged over Andrew, what if someone was trying to take advantage of her or something worse. His foot pressed harder on the accelerator and within ten minutes he was parked and on his way in to find her.

It didn't take him long to find her sitting at a bar stool taking shots. She toasted to the bartender, "To you, my good bar-keep! Keep them a 'coming." The bartender just laughed, shaking his head as he walked away. Andrew watched her take the shot then noticed she looked quite woozy and a bit green. He quickly walked up to her, putting his hand on her arm, making her jump so bad, she fell off the stool and on the ground hard. She started to cry when she looked up at him with her dark, forest eyes.

"Great." He groaned. "I'm sorry, I didn't mean to scare you, but I think it's time to go sweetie." Andrew said in a soft voice, extending his hand so he could help her off the ground.

Unfortunately for him, this made her cry more. "I don't want to go..." she whined, wiping her face and smearing her makeup. Andrew had to admit even though she was a mess, she was still breathtaking in the dim light setting. He kept his hand extended and she reluctantly took it.

"When I asked you to come here tonight, I didn't mean come and babysit me. You think you can just waltz in here looking delicious and just expect me to fall into your arms?" She groaned as she wobbly stood on her feet. "I mean come on look at you! You could be a sex god with your damn grey shirt and your chest hair...No man could ever compete with you!" she admitted as she brought her hand to his chest to keep her balance. Andrew heard her swallow loudly as she touched him, sending electricity through his core. He was doing everything in his power not to just sweep her up in his arms and take her back to his place, bring her right into his bedroom to ravish her. If she wanted a sex god he knew he had no problem fulfilling that for her, gladly. The way she was talking to him and the aroma of vanilla body spray was definitely turning him on and his body temperature was rising far too fast for his liking.

"Andrew, why do you have to smell so good?" she asked leaning her nose in by his collarbone, slowly raising her head to the curvature of his chin. She stopped at his ear, slowly turning her head toward him. Once their eyes met he felt as if he got struck by a semi in his stomach and groin. Her eyes burst with gold, radiating with the dark, rich green. Her intense stare, shook his core and he felt that his mind and body was suspended in time. Her hands drifted from his hand up his arm. Her finger tips lightly danced over his chest and slowly made their way down his stomach. Her fingertips scorched his skin with lingering touches. He groaned as he grabbed her hand that now lingered down his pants, stopping her before both of them would make a terrible mistake.

"Okay time to go..." he said, taking her hand and dragging her from the bar, to get her purse.

"Wait, let me say goodbye to Rachel and Benjamin..." she said trailing off as they both found them in the crowd kissing. Andrew's grip on Eleanor's hand became tighter. His heart sunk in his chest for her. He could see tears form on the edge of her eyes. She dropped his hand, grabbed her things and then rushed out the door. Andrew quickly was on her tail, not letting her out of his sight. Once they both got outside, Eleanor stumbled in the freshness of the cool night air. Andrew grabbed Eleanor's shoulders so she could steady herself. He helped her over to a bench where she put her head into her hands. Andrew sat down quietly next to her, he had no idea what to really do or say to her. He was still trying to cool down himself from her words inside. He knew that she was thinking of seeing Benjamin and Rachel kiss and he planned on having a few choice words with him on Monday.

"I am acting like an idiot, aren't I?" she mumbled, still looking down at the ground.

Andrew slowly placed his hand on her lower thigh, "No, but you're drunk and not thinking clearly."

She sniffled and sat up, turning to look at him, her eyes her red and puffy, her makeup smeared even more than before. "Why did you break up with Becca?"

Andrew groaned. "Is this the best time to be asking me this?"

She sniffled again, wiping the tears away from her face, "I think it's a perfect time."

Andrew stiffened and anger pumped through his blood. He really didn't want to tell her the reason why, since she was part of that reason.

He snapped. "I broke up with her because she cheated on me. I don't know for how long or truly how many...she told me after when she thought I did..." he admitted turning away from her, so she couldn't see his face. His fists were clenched between his legs. He tried to take a deep breath, hoping it would calm his nerves.

She asked confused, "Why would she think you cheated? Did you? I mean- you wouldn't you are way better than that...I'm sorry I even asked. You don't have to tell me."

Andrew turned his head and looked ahead of him, staring at the pavement. He was afraid to meet her eyes after he knew what he was going to admit, "Because I said your name while we were having sex."

Andrew peeked at her from the corner of his eye as she didn't say anything. She turned her head from him, staring out ahead of her, processing what he just told her.

He sighed, looking down at his hands. "In a way I felt I did cheat on her... even though it's not to the same extent of what she did..." Andrew looked at her this time, hoping she would say something. She turned toward him, her expression unreadable.

"I'm sorry," she responded.

He looked at her dumbfounded. "That's it?"

She looked angry. "What do you mean, that's it? What am I supposed to say? I am sorry she cheated on you, Andrew. I really am because you're an amazing man and any woman would be lucky to have you. But if you want me to say I feel excited that you said my name while you were having sex with someone else? Well...I'm not."

Andrew was shocked by her statement and also a little hurt. In a way, he thought by saying that to her, she could maybe get a sense that he had feelings for her, but he realized now that was probably not the best way to do it. She stood up, putting her jacket on and flinging her purse over her shoulder.

"Where do you think you're going?" Andrew exclaimed grabbing her hand, pulling her toward him.

"I'm walking home," she snapped, yanking his hand away.

"Let me give you a ride," he suggested, taking her hand again. Andrew couldn't help but like the feel of her hand in his.

"No, I can walk home. I don't live that far...please," she reassured him.

Andrew closed the distance between them, taking his finger to lift her chin up to meet his eyes. Her eyes went wide as she looked away from his stare. He knew she was holding back unseen forces that scattered throughout her mind. He clenched his jaw. "Please look at me. I'm sorry about everything tonight, for what I said or didn't say...for what you saw before back in there."

She huffed. "It was bound to happen. Everyone leaves me. I was meant to be alone...I know that now."

"Why would you say that?" he said, pulling her even closer to him, her hand resting on his chest. He could sense her trying to lean away, but she didn't tell him to let go.

"My mother left me... my grandma and family left me, and you will leave me... These scars are my curse. " She insisted, pulling and turning away from him as she wiped her tears away.

"Eleanor..." he sighed, reaching for her hand again. His chest ached in pain for what she was going through. He wanted to do everything in his power to protect her, to make sure she would never feel this way again.

She sighed loudly. "Fine, take me home? There's no point in fighting with you," she said looking up at him with tears rolling down her cheeks. Andrew nodded with a tormented gaze. They headed for his truck, Andrew's mind plagued of all the things of tonight.

They headed to her house in silence. He could feel

the tension in the cab of his truck. Andrew pulled into the driveway, shutting off the engine once he parked. They sat like that for what felt like an eternity. The tension became even thicker, hot ribbons swirling around them as beads of sweat formed on his forehead.

"Thank you for the ride..." she said taking the seat belt off, opening up the door. He grabbed her hand, making her turn her head toward him. He wanted so bad to grab her arms, heave her over to his side of the truck and kiss her as if their lives depended on it. The pain in her eyes remained the same; her pouty lips form a line, and her breathing became heavy.

"Eleanor, I will never leave you...I promise you that," Andrew said letting go of her hand, reaching up to caress her face. If he couldn't kiss, her he had to at least touch her, to feel her close or feel connected to her in some way. She grew stiff for a moment but then melted into his hand and he watched a tear roll down her cheek, landing on his palm. It felt like the world was crashing down around him, he knew he was falling for her.

She gave him a weak smile. "Goodnight Andrew..." she whispered as she kept her head there a moment longer. Sadly, she slowly climbed out of the truck and sluggishly headed toward the door, looking at him one last time before she headed inside. As he drove home, he yearned to prove that she was more than her damaged heart and scars.

CHAPTER TEN

Eleanor woke up as the sun poured into her bedroom. She groaned, looking at the clock. She sighed, rolling over on her back and covering her head with her arm, trying to stop the pounding in her head from the pressing issues that raced through her mind. The way Andrew's eyes bore into hers as he said the powerful declaration. He had a way of saying more with his body than his words last night. She melted whenever he touched her. The stress left her body like a fog lifting over a meadow. Her walls seemed to get weaker every time she saw him. She liked it, but it still terrified her. What if she let him fully in and then he broke her heart. She knew she would never be able to fully heal.

She chuckled on how foolish she was even texting him last night, especially since she was drinking. Cringing at how ridiculous she acted, she couldn't see what he saw in her. She knew she would go crazy if she lay there anymore thinking about it, so she sluggishly got up and headed for the kitchen to pour a cup of hot coffee.

She melted, sipping the savory aroma of mocha; her nerves and limbs became alive and she felt somewhat human again. After the caffeine kick, she got dressed and decided to head out and explore more of the town. She opened her front door to get the paper when she noticed a flyer on the front of it saying something about the Botanical Garden. Eleanor gasped; she wasn't aware there was one in Hope Harbor. She smiled decidedly; that would be exactly what she would do today.

The coastal Botanical Garden was located on the outer edge of Hope Harbor, with trails overlooking the water's edge. The two-hundred-fifty acre space had ten different varieties of gardens to explore. Eleanor was ecstatic at the thought of spending the day in the vast gardens filled with beautiful and exotic flowers. It was more than a perfect day, sunny with a little wind. She wore a long spring dress, sandals and a soft blue cardigan.

Eleanor started in the Van Gogh Garden. There was an abundance of flowers that tickled not just the eyes but the senses. Eleanor had never experienced an overwhelming aroma of flora that consumed her body. She walked down by the fountain, across the artistically done rustic wooden bridge. She got over the bridge and noticed a group of older teenagers by the pond where they were busy drawing the scenery around them. One of the boys stood out to her with familiarity. As if he could sense her looking at him, he looked up at her.

"Ellie!" he shouted, getting off the stone and running up to her giving her a big hug.

Her heart swelled in her chest. "Trevor! It's been way too long!" she said, squeezing him tighter.

He took her hand and led her to the group making everyone look and take notice. A lady around Eleanor's age with strawberry blonde hair and blue eyes greeted Eleanor when Trevor dropped her hand to go grab his painting.

"May I ask what is this group is?" Eleanor asked, intrigued, looking around at all the ages of the people in the group.

"This is a non-profit organization that connects younger teens and adults with special needs. It's a place where they can come to learn, grow, and create with each other," She smiled proudly.

"That is amazing! Would you mind if I stayed for a while and talked to Trevor more?"

Her eyes crinkled kindly and her smile widened. "Please do. It isn't often that we have visitors but I know they would absolutely love it! I'm Kim by the way, if you need anything," she said, moving to the side, gesturing toward the group of kids in a circle on the grass.

"Thank you! I'm Eleanor." She replied, following behindKim.

"Guys, we have a special surprise visitor today, her name is Eleanor. Please give her a warm friendly welcome," she exclaimed, excitedly.

"Hi Eleanor!" the group said in unison, making her giggle. Trevor ran back up, handing Eleanor a picture that he was working on of the pond. She was impressed by the vast amount of colors that he used for the plants and the texture he added to the pond. She thought it was simply incredible. "Trevor, would you draw a picture for me sometime? You're very good and I love this one." She smiled at him.

Trevor beamed as big as Eleanor had ever seen him smile. She could tell he was very proud of his work. "I would love to!" he chimed, clapping his hands together. He grabbed her hand again and made her sit down next to him. Both became silent, wrapped up in their drawings.

Trevor stopped coloring and just stared at Eleanor. She could sense his eyes and looked up towards him. "Why are you so sad, Ellie?"

She sighed, giving him a weak smile, "What makes you say that?"

"Your eyes aren't sparkling today," he replied.

She kept smiling, even though inside her heart was breaking. "Oh, Trevor...you know me so well. I'm just sad, but it's okay. I will get better soon."

"You look like Andy, when he dropped me off this morning," Trevor frowned.

Eleanor sighed, her heart breaking more. She couldn't imagine what Andrew must be going through and she knew that she didn't help the matter at all last night. She felt horrible that he had to come because of her drunken stupidity. She knew that she had to apologize and make it up to him somehow, but how?

"Eleanor, what are you doing here?" Andrew asked, as he looked down at her sitting next to Trevor, both of them drawing. She jumped as she looked up, shielding her eyes from the sun's rays. He was captivated by her beauty once more. Her hair shimmered red in the sunlight, her toned legs peeking from under her dress, and her voluptuous breasts tantalizing him through the top. Wild images bolted through his mind of them rolling around in the grass under a tree, lying naked, panting as he made her moan his name. Their hands roaming each other's bodies, Andrew devouring her over and over, never getting his fill of her.

"Andrew! Hi, um...yeah, I found out about this place today and wanted to check it out. You know me and flowers...can't get enough," she rambled, turning her head away hiding the blush that crept cross her face. Trevor spotted me and we've been talking and coloring ever since," she replied.

"That's nice of you. Trevor did you have a good time with Eleanor?" he asked bending down to Trevor's eye level.

Trevor looked up at him, searching in Andrew's eyes for something, then back at Eleanor who was looking perplexed and then back to Andrew, looking intensely at both of them. After what Andrew thought was a grueling minute, Trevor smiled like he seemed to find what he was looking for.

"Yes," he smiled brightly.

Andrew's mouth gaped, choking out a laugh, in complete shock. He had been waiting for this moment for over a year. "What?"

"Yes, I did," Trevor replied again, trying to reassure Andrew.

Andrew was so happy; he placed his hand on Trevor's shoulder, laughing more as tears rolled down his face. He couldn't believe this day had come. He wrapped his arms around Trevor, holding him tight as tears flowed down his face.

"Thank you." Andrew smiled. "I love you buddy." The darkness had finally lifted and the sun shone through to his heart. His chest ached with happiness. He wrapped his hand around Trevor's head bringing him closer, crying in Trevor's hair. He pulled Trevor back, and with his hands on each side of Trevor's face, he smiled brightly at him. Trevor just grinned back at him.

"I'm sorry," Trevor finally said. "That I have hurt you. I love you."

Tears threatened Andrew's eyes again. "Don't be sorry Trevor, you grieved in your own way," Andrew hugged Trevor once more to make sure it wasn't a dream.

Andrew caught Eleanor's eyes and he could see they were gleaming with tears, as she smiled brightly. Her hands were enclosed over her heart. He pulled back from the hug and wrapped his arm around Trevor's shoulder. He wanted nothing more than to be finally close to his brother after the grueling year they had.

They walked to the parking lot in silence. Ideally enough for Andrew, he realized he parked right next to Eleanor. Trevor got in, but Andrew and Eleanor both hesitated from their driver's side looking at each other.

"I am really glad you're here Eleanor..." he paused, catching his breath. "I would like to talk to you about the other night and few other things. Will you have dinner with me on Friday?" he asked, holding his breath, praying that she would say yes.

Eleanor looked down, studying the pavement as Andrew waited nervously. His breath and pulse quickened. There was nothing more he wanted to do then to see her again and after his lack of sleep last night, even after an ice cold shower, he couldn't shake off the previous events. He spent the whole morning thinking about his situation and how he felt about Eleanor. After a painstakingly long minute, she looked up with her expression unreadable.

"Yes, I would like that." She smiled faintly. He couldn't imagine what was going through her mind, but he hoped on Friday that she would able to tell him. Unfortunately, now he had to wait a whole week just to find out, but it would give him enough time to focus on how he was going to tell her exactly how he felt about her.

CHAPTER ELEVEN

"Eleanor, we need to talk!" Rachel shouted from the other side of Eleanor's door, pounding it continuously. Eleanor glanced at her clock and groaned.

"What on earth does she want at eight in the morning?" she muttered to herself. "This had better be good!" Eleanor shouted as she sluggishly put on her robe, dragging her feet to the door. She opens the door feeling and probably looking, half dead.

"Good morning, beautiful!" Rachel chimed, moving the door wide, letting herself in. Eleanor was too tired to even object. She turned around to watch Rachel bring in two cups of coffee and a white bag containing bakery goodies. Eleanor shrugged. If she was bringing food, there was no way she was going to shoo Rachel out of her house.

"What brings you here so early?" Eleanor yawned, as she plopped down in the chair, smelling the delicious aroma of warm sugar and glaze. Rachel didn't say anything, just got out the donuts and handed her the coffee. Eleanor couldn't help but be quizzical about Rachel's demeanor. Once Rachel got everything out she sat down across from Eleanor, locking eyes with her.

"Did you hear about Andrew and Becca." Rachel started rambling. Eleanor stopped her by putting her finger to Rachel's mouth to silence her.

"He told me," she stated glumly.

Rachel looked confused, raising her eyebrow, "So let me get this straight, he told you and you aren't at least relieved that, he isn't going to marry her!...And not at least flustered that he thought of you when he was naked and horny?" Rachel asked, taking a bite of her donut, her eyes filled of bewilderment, wiggling her eyebrows.

Eleanor couldn't help but chuckle while she shook her head. "Ha! Easier said than done."

Rachel's shoulders slumped and she frowned. "Aw, Elle, can I be honest? I have seen the marks. I know you try your best to hide them, but we have all seen them at the store. You don't have to tell me until you're ready, but you're a woman that has hormones, just like me. You can't deny there isn't some attraction toward him."

Eleanor didn't want to admit it, but Rachel was right. She was frightened that people talked about her burns, but there was nothing much she could do about it now.

"What am I supposed to do, Rachel? I am stuck between a rock and a hard place." Eleanor groaned, laying her head down against the table.

"You know what you need to do...tell him. Everything happens for a reason, Elle. Maybe this is your chance to find true love!" Rachel smiled brightly, rubbing her hand on Eleanor's arm, reassuring her. Eleanor took a big gulp of her coffee. Eleanor didn't know which she should be more afraid of. Telling

Andrew the truth, or realizing the truth herself, that she could be in love with him.

Friday came without a hitch and sure enough she was standing inside O'Malley's waiting for her host to come and bring her to the table where Andrew would be waiting for her. She thought Friday would never come and without seeing or hearing from Andrew besides his text on location and time, she couldn't help but feel anxious.

She followed the waitress to a wooden deck that overlooked the bay. Her eyes scanned the room and met Andrew's instantly. He stood up as she approached. Her mouth went dry as he stood there in front of her, stoically handsome. Her inner thighs began to tingle and she pressed them together to control it. He stood there in blue jeans that hung loose on his hips, a white t-shirt with a button down light blue jean shirt. His hair was ruffled, creating curls around his face, emphasizing his high cheek bones. He looked so beautiful but worn, making her sad to see such a beautiful man looked exhausted as he tried to hide it behind his grin.

"Hello, Eleanor, thank you for meeting me," he smiled, pulling out her chair. She blushed as he turned toward her and sat down next to her.

"Of course, but I need to say something first," she paused. "Are we here because of the other night?" she asked, looking down flustered. Sighing, she looked back up at him, smiling shyly. "I am so sorry for how I acted. I never drink and I had no idea that I would act like a raging hormonal teenage girl." She chuckled nervously, biting her nails.

She heard him chuckle as well, turning back to see his face redden, rubbing his hands through his hair. "No, that isn't why. It was unexpected, but you weren't the only one that was worried about acting like a horny teenager," he replied, with flirtatious flames form in his eyes.

A current went through her whole body and the pit of her stomach turned, as heat rose through her body. He stared intently into her eyes, feeling that her body was going to burst.

He coughed, breaking the spell, and he looked away as if to clear his head. He turned back with a boyish grin on his face; as if he knew what he was doing to her.

"The reason I asked you to come meet me is because I have the next three weeks off for vacation. I know you mentioned fixing your house, and I think this would be a perfect time for me to help you. I could start working on it while you are at work and then the days you have off you can help me. What do you say? I have to start using my tools that I finally got out of the clutter in the shed, they have been building up dust." He chuckled.

She was so surprised. This was the last thing she thought he would want to talk about. Why he would want to help her? "You would really do this for me? I will pay for everything including labor..." she added.

"No, you don't need to pay me, please I want to do this for you..." he interrupted her, placing his hand on hers.

"Why?" she asked curiously, as he gazed into her eyes, his eyebrows furrowed. His eyes seemed to be pleading with hers. "What can I do to make it up to you?" she asked, seeing that he wouldn't give up and she squeezed his hand, making him smile.

"You've been through so much Eleanor. Knowing that Maine is your home now, I want to make your home something special for you. What kind of things do you need done?" he asked, pulling out a napkin and pen.

She chuckled. "You're really serious about this? Umm... well okay, I have actually been working on it quite a bit. I painted the outside of the house and I have been working on the bushes, but I lack the proper equipment. So the bushes in front of the house, and I want the brick wall gone in the front. The flower patches have to be weeded, but you don't have to do that and this is just for the outside at least...the inside is a different story."

As she watched him intently write everything down, she said, "Andrew."

She waited until he looked up at her. "You gave me your reasons for doing this for me, but what about you? You're hurting, but yet you're helping me. I feel that I am the one who should be helping you. I can't help but feel I am responsible..." she said, trailing off.

He set down the pen and looked at her with perplexed eyes. "You're not the reason for our break up, that was all her. Yes, I said I was thinking about you when we were in bed, but it wouldn't have mattered if you were here or not. I should be thanking you. I would have married her, given her my whole heart while she would have given herself to another man."

"I don't deserve it..." she muttered, quietly.

"Then I will just have to prove it to you," he replied, clearly upset but determined.

"How?" she snipped, taking a drink of her water. This is not how she thought this was going to turn out.

"You want to know how to pay me back for working on your house? Go on one date with me," he replied, jaw clenched, line forming on his forehead, serious.

Eleanor eyes widened and her mouth dropped, dumbstruck. "What? Are you serious?"

He looked surprised. "Yes, why would that be a shock for you?" he asked studying her with his piercing blue eyes, taking in all her movements and expressions.

She shook her head looking down quickly replying. "No...I mean... you just got out of a three year relationship..." She said, trailing off, trying to avoid his eye contact. Her heart screaming yes as it tried to pound out of her chest.

"Yes. I did, but I realized that I did myself a favor and I thought long and hard about this Eleanor. Why are you pushing me away?" he snapped, his eyebrows scrunched together and his eyes immersed in anger.

"It's better this way..." she whispered quietly, trying to hold back the eruption of tears that were threatening to fall from her eyes.

"Better? I don't understand. We have come so far, you told me your secret and I promise I would never let anyone hurt you. Please don't push me away. Don't you think it hurts, you rejecting me?" He asked quietly, his eyes piercing right through her. She looked down and tried to find the right words to say.

What was she supposed to say, that she was falling in love with him and was scared? Was she overreacting because it was just one date? Was she even ready to really date someone with this magnitude of feelings that she had for him?

"Eleanor, please...why? Can't you at least give me a reason why?" he badgered, leaning in toward her so he wouldn't make a scene in public. She got up from her seat, glaring at him as fury shot through her. She didn't need to be treated like this and out of all people, he should have understood.

She shook her head. "And you think I'm pushy...Why are you pushing me into this? For crying out loud, I said no to Benjamin. What makes you think I could go on a date with you! Especially you..." she said growing quiet. "Maybe...just maybe did it ever occur to you that I could be..." She paused, getting up from the table, wiping a tear away. She wasn't going to cry in front of him, not now. "I could be falling for you and it scares the shit out of me!" she whispered sharply, looking into his shocked eyes. Without another glance, she walked away from the table storming off through the restaurant.

CHAPTER TWELVE

"Okay, man, what's wrong? You have been in a fog for the past couple days. Come on, talk to me." Ryan said, while Andrew sat across from him at the local diner during their lunch break. Ryan always had a high temper and was kind of a player with the ladies, but whenever Andrew needed him, he was there, a true Irishmen at heart. "Does this have to do with Becca? It's been a couple months, do yourself a favor. She was no good for you." Ryan leaned over, patting Andrews arm.

Andrew didn't feel like talking. He didn't really feel like doing much of anything. He kept replaying the conversation between him and Eleanor. He was frustrated at her, but also at himself for pushing her. He knew better. He groaned. "No...it's not about Becca. I am done and over her."

"Then what...?" Ryan asked, glancing at Andrew waiting for a response.

Andrew groaned. "You're as nosy as a woman!"

"Ha! So it is about a woman?" Ryan pointed his finger in Andrews face. Andrew waved his hand away, but red crept over his face. "Your blushing isn't helping your situation. You're making it more obvious." He laughed.

Andrew groaned again, taking a drink of his cola. "Fine...why can't you just let me sulk?"

"Like hell! I already know who it is! I am smarter

than I let you think I am. I didn't want to bruise your ego. You know, you being the smart one and me being the sexy one," he gloated, as he leaned back in his chair stretching, flexing his bicep as a young blonde waitress walked past, and trying to catch her eye.

Andrew shook his head in disbelief. "You are so full of shit! Well, since you are so smart, who do you think I am talking about?" he asked, looking Ryan dead in the eye. He wished his feelings toward Eleanor weren't so damn obvious. He wasn't sure himself. He knew that there was a force that pulled him toward her whenever she was near and an undeniable ache when she left. He knew damn well he was falling for her. It bothered him that here he was taking a big leap of faith by asking her out, and she couldn't even meet him half way.

"Eleanor. Don't think I don't notice when you casually bring up her name. You have it bad Andrew. You weren't even like this with Becca," Ryan confessed, leaning in toward Andrew. Andrew put his head in his hands, his elbows leaning on the table. He ran his hands through his hair over and over, just trying to think what to do. He had no idea that he did it.

"What happened with her?" Ryan asked. "I'm all ears, no more playing around. You obviously have strong feelings for her."

Andrew took a deep breath, feeling his chest compress just thinking of her. "We got into a fight a couple of days ago. I asked her if I could help fix her house up, she asked me how she could repay me, so I told her to go on a date with me and she said no. Didn't even think about it, I just don't understand." Andrew clenched his fist onto the table angrily. He groaned, "It didn't help that I pressured her into telling me why she wouldn't. I should have known better than to do that...

but when she finally told me..." Andrew stopped dead in his tracks. His eyes widened and his heart pounded. Her response never clicked until now. A shift rocked through his whole body, a warm sensation radiating through every pore in his skin, his throat tightening. His heart raced. How come he didn't think of this before? How could he have missed those crucial words?

"What? What did she say?" Ryan asked frantically, intrigued.

Andrew sighed as a faint smile crossed his face. "Because she was scared she was falling in love with me. I am dumb. I'm really dumb...shit. Why couldn't I think of that before now?" He smacked his forehead.

"I have to go," Andrew declared, abruptly standing up to grab his coat. His mind was racing and he had to get back to his house to start planning what needed to be done.

"Where are you going?" Ryan asked, confused.

"I have a house to go work on," Andrew smiled at Ryan as he threw down money for his food. Ryan smirked, shaking his head. "Go get her Andrew." Andrew laughed as he walked out of the diner, because that's exactly what he was intending to do.

Andrew got what he needed and headed over to Eleanor's house. First order of business was tearing down that brick wall in front with the bushes. Thankfully she was at work; he didn't know how much work he would be able to do if she were home. He took off his button down shirt, leaving his white tank on. He grabbed gloves and his sledge hammer and headed to the front. He was actually excited about this; he could finally let out the pent up emotion that had been churning inside him for months.

He swung back, slamming the sledge into the side

of the wall, using all the strength he had in his body. The sledge hit the wall as an intense vibration went up his arms into his whole body. Huge chunks of rock crumbled and fell onto the ground. It felt liberating to him that his strength could withstand a wall of rock. He knew he had to stop thinking and just keep hitting.

After an hour of constant hits, Andrew had enough and knew it was time for a break. He was drenched in sweat, taking off his shirt and using it to wipe off his face. He went back to the trunk and grabbed his water taking a sip then pouring some over his body to cool off. Wiping his face off, he stood motionless as that familiar force pulled through his body once again. He turned slowly to see her there.

"Eleanor," he said breathlessly.

Eleanor gasped, her eyes glued on the magnificent, gorgeous, half-naked body, covered in sweat, his chest glistening in the sun. She swallowed hard, her mouth dry, throat tight. She bit her lip as he stared back intensely, his lips formed a thin line, hands clenched. His expression was unreadable, his body stiff. Her loins erupted in tingling sensation and her hunger for him grew tremendously. She wanted him, bad.

Her mind was fighting with her heart. "Don't do it, he could hurt you," she took a deep breath, never took her eyes off him.

She met him in four strides, without a word, she took her hands and grabbed his face, her lips meeting his. She thought there was no better way to show him how she felt than by doing this. As soon as their lips met, her body erupted into a fire of hunger and lust. His mouth was stiff at first, but then seemed to relax and mold to hers perfectly. She had never tasted anything so intoxicating, sweet as honey. Andrew's fingers intertwined in Eleanor's hair, pulling her deeper into the kiss. Her hands roamed his whole body, feeling every muscle, every curve. She didn't care if he was sweaty; she wanted him to take her out of her clothes. He lifted her up, pulling her closer to him, though that wasn't nearly close enough for her. He lifted her onto the front of his truck, frantically opening her willing legs as he stood in front of her.

"Andrew," she groaned, in his mouth.

One word made him freeze. He removed his hands from her and pulled away panting, trying to catch his breath. Eleanor blinked fast thinking her mind blank. She touched her hand to her mouth to feel the light tenderness of his lips. Her heart just screamed. "Did I really just kiss him?" her mind raced. "What did I just do?" She felt her body get heavy. She'd never felt such a powerful sensation consume her. It confused her, she didn't know whether to do it again or cry. She felt so vulnerable that she could shatter in a million pieces. She fell to her knees, with her head in her hands and sobbed. In moments, she felt strong arms wrap around her.

"Shh...please don't cry, Eleanor. You didn't do anything wrong. This is new to you," he whispered his voice raspy in her ear. She shook her head in disagreement. She was exposed, scared, and confused at the same time. During the kiss she felt alive, her body hummed with excitement.

"Is this how it really feels?" she asked, her whole body shaking. "What do you feel Eleanor?" he asked, instead of answering her question. He pulled her out of her huddled position so he could see her face. His strong hands cradling her head, his eyes locked with hers. She sighed, wanting to break his gaze but she couldn't look away from his probing gaze. His pupils dilated and she could tell he was still breathing heavily. If she didn't know any better she thought he was nervous for her answer.

"Honestly, I feel scared, exposed, and vulnerable," she paused as she noticed his eyes grow soft and even a little sad. She went on with a smirk, "Warm, alive, and secure."

His shoulders dropped as he let out his breath. He smiled warmly at her and it made her toes curl. He wrapped her back into his arms, never taking his eyes off her face, constantly watching for any sign of fear. At that point, Eleanor's body seemed to react with want, not fear to Andrew's touch. When she felt the warmth from his body she let out a big sigh.

Andrew couldn't help but chuckle a bit. "Are you comfortable? You didn't seem to tense up when I touched you. What changed?" he asked, curiously.

Eleanor grinned back at him. His smile was infectious. "When you kissed me back, I guess you broke the last piece to the wall down. I think I am starting to finally let go,"

Andrew smiled brighter. "That is the most romantic thing, any girl has said to me," he chuckled, nuzzling his face into her neck. She could hear him smelling her hair.

"I hate to break this up but...I don't know what to do now. I have never been in any sort of relationship before," she said, her face reddening.

He searched her eyes. "We take this," gesturing between him and Eleanor, "slow. I don't care how slow we take this, Elle. I have wanted to be with you since the first moment I met you. I know I was with Becca, but I figured that once Becca and I were married, my feelings for you would disappear. But fate was with us and here we are," he wrapped his arms tighter around Eleanor. "It would have never worked out between Becca and I no matter how I tried. Her father was against me from the get go and we were never on the same page. What we have here and will have in the future, I wouldn't trade for anything in the world." Andrew said, with a huge grin flashing across his face, making his dimples appear.

CHAPTER THIRTEEN

"Amelia, is that you?" Eleanor asked, picking up the phone. Eleanor had just sat down at her kitchen table with Andrew for supper, taking a break from working outside. After their talk, Eleanor decided she could at least help him with the outside work and make supper for him. After an emotional, but triumphant day, she was ready for it to end. A call from her favorite cousin from back home was a welcome distraction.

"Yes!! Hi honey! How are you? Is everything going okay there? Are there any cute men? I miss you! What are you up too?" Amelia rambled, alerting Eleanor that something was wrong.

"Yes everything is good. I am enjoying dinner with one of the cute men here," Eleanor said, winking at Andrew. "Amelia, what's wrong? You seem worked up about something."

Eleanor could hear Amelia's breathing pick up, letting out a great sigh. "I'm in Maine."

Eleanor dropped her burger, rushed out of her chair, and started to pace. "What do you mean you're in Maine? Where? Are you okay, honey?" Eleanor asked.

"Yes I am okay. I am in Freedom Point. Do you think you could come get me?" Amelia cried. Eleanor's heart sank. A million thoughts ran through Eleanor's mind, but one major one came to mind, her damn uncle. If he hurt her, there would be a price to pay.

"Hold tight Amelia, we're on our way," Eleanor said, Andrew already grabbing his keys and heading to the door. Eleanor quickly grabbed her things and headed out with him. She would do everything in her power to make sure Amelia was safe and well. She was the only one from her family she could trust now. She wouldn't let anything stand in their way.

Andrew couldn't help but notice how fidgety Eleanor was on the twenty minute drive to Freedom Point. He reached across the cab and slowly took her hand, making sure not to scare her. She jumped a little, looking down at their hands then back up to him. He could see the tension melt away. Her shoulders relaxed a little, but he did notice her chewing on her nails. A nervous habit, he thought.

"What on earth do you think she could be doing here? Don't get me wrong I am excited to see her. It's been six months. If everything were alright she would have told me she was coming. This has to do with my uncle. I just know it," she exclaimed, huffing, turning to look out the window.

Andrew wasn't really sure what to say, "We will find out soon enough. At least she was able to come to you in her time of need. Maybe she just needed to get away." He said trying to reassure her. As they pulled up in front of Freedom Point Airport, Eleanor got out of the truck before Andrew could put it into park. He watched her run in front of the truck and across the street to where

Amelia was waiting. As soon as Amelia saw Eleanor she dropped her luggage she was carrying, and rushed to Eleanor hugging her tightly. She had three huge suitcases, besides the duffle bag. Something told Andrew that she was planning on more than just a visit.

"He has what?" Eleanor shrieked, setting down her coffee, afraid that she would spill it with the news she just received. Andrew moved from his chair and sat next to Eleanor putting his hand on her knee trying to calm her trembling hand. Andrew knotted his other hand into a fist. He had an undeniable urge to hit something...more like someone.

"When I was snooping through his phone, I saw a strange text and sure enough he had been talking to your mother. He told her everything about Claire's will. It didn't say he had plans or anything though. As soon as I saw that I knew I had to come see you. The things they were saying..." she trailed off, as tears formed in her eyes. "This is so not fair, you didn't do anything to them," she whimpered.

It was Eleanor's turn to do the comforting. She broke from Andrew's embrace and cradled Amelia. Eleanor turned to Andrew with a worried look. Her face seemed to age right before him. Hard lines formed on her forehead and dark circles that Andrew hadn't seen before seemed to appear under her emerald eyes. Sadly, he could also sense the wall he had tried so hard to knock down slowly reappear around Eleanor.

"Amelia," Eleanor sighed, making Amelia lift her head as she sniffed. "Your dad came to visit me, two months ago," Andrew sighed, rubbing his hand through his hair as he leaned back onto the couch as Eleanor told Amelia the story about her father's visit.

Eleanor woke up early, making sure not to wake

Amelia who slept next to her in the queen size bed. Neither one got much sleep last night. Andrew stayed as long as he could before Ryan called saying he had to leave to get some sleep before they both headed out onto the water with his dad. Eleanor noticed Andrew didn't say much, but she saw that his fists never loosened their grip through the whole night. Eleanor's heart broke for Amelia as she had to relay the horrible story of her own father. Amelia couldn't fathom why the money from the will meant so much to her father.

Eleanor was happy for Amelia to be here. It felt like a little part of her, the hole in heart closed up as soon as they were reunited. They always had a special bond growing up, though they didn't get to see each other much. They were more like sisters than cousins. They could always rely on each other. Amelia had always tried her best to spend her free days at her grandma's house just so she could be together with Claire and Eleanor.

Eleanor poured a hot cup of coffee and headed to the table, where she stared out at the water. "May I join you?" Amelia asked, as she shuffled sleepily into the kitchen.

"Of course, would you like some coffee?" Eleanor asked.

Amelia nodded, sitting down at the table.

"This place is so beautiful. No wonder you wanted to move here," Amelia said sighing. Eleanor joined her at the table, setting down the coffee and creamer. "Thank you."

"Claire was the one who sent me here. I found a postcard in the chest she left me. It was sent here from a woman named Mary, which I found out was Andrew's mother. He actually called me after Claire passed. He wanted to talk to her because he found a photograph that linked his mother to Claire. We've been trying to put the pieces together since both aren't here anymore. Believe me, since I moved here I have been put to the test. Everyone has been so kind, wanting to be in each other's lives. That is definitely something I am not used to. And with Andrew…" Eleanor chuckled. "From the first moment I met him, he had struck a chord in me. He pushed all my buttons, trying to get close to me. I felt compelled by him, even if it scared the crap out of me at first." Eleanor confided. Eleanor didn't have to relay her horrible past growing up with Amelia because they shared everything with one another.

"It looks to me like he is in love with you. He was pretty quiet yesterday, is he usually that quiet?"

"No, he isn't. I just think with what he heard yesterday and first-hand experience dealing with your father, Andrew senses that your dad is going to try and do something again," Eleanor explained, continuing to tell Amelia everything that had happened to her since arriving in Maine.

"Eleanor, I believe you moving here was the best thing for you. I can't imagine what might have happened if you had stayed in Wisconsin. You have become so much stronger," Amelia smiled, reaching across the table, touching her hand. Eleanor placed her hand on top of Amelia's. "Eleanor." She began in a serious tone. "I want to stay here." Her eyes teared up, worrying Eleanor. "I can't go back home. Not after what my father has done. Since he found out about the money, that is all he can think about. My mother," she scoffed. "All she cares about is material things. They honestly wouldn't care if I left. Bob and Stanley are going to college in a couple of months and I highly doubt they will come home. Our family isn't a family anymore. My parents are so wrapped up in greed," Amelia cried.

Eleanor's heart broke for Amelia. She thought they were a happy family growing up. Seeing Amelia break down, made Eleanor more worried about just what Amelia had gone through before she got here. "Have you tried to talk to them?"

Tears rolled down Amelia's face. She shook her head. "I tried, countless times, but nothing...just nothing...please, Eleanor" Amelia begged.

Eleanor squeezed her hand. "Of course, stay as long as you need. I have a spare room that is all yours!"

"Elle, I want to move here. I don't want to return. I will get a job and start my life here. There is nothing to go back to," Amelia said, her brows puckered up in dismay.

"Don't rush into anything. Just think about it, but if in the end that is what you want to do, I fully support it. I could get you a job at the flower shop if you like?" Eleanor asked. Amelia didn't look too convinced- she just shrugged, wiping away her tears. "How about this? Later on today, I can show you around Hope Harbor and if someplace strikes you in work, just let me know."

"Thank you Eleanor, that means the world to me!" Amelia smiled.

Even though Andrew had off, the next day he stopped down on the dock to help Ryan and his dad pack up for their lobster trip around the tip of Maine. Andrew wanted to go with them this year, but didn't want to leave Trevor for so long. It did, however, give him a better excuse to have off and spend some time with

Trevor and Eleanor.

The sun was high up in the sky, making it one of the hottest days they had so far in Maine. Beads of sweat ran down his face as he hauled out the lobster traps, making sure they were nice and clean, ready to be baited when they left for their journey. The breeze off the Gulf was the only thing keeping Andrew cool. Out of the corner of his eye, he sensed movement coming down the dock. As he looked up, he put his hand over his eyes to shield the sun.

"Hello! Is this Paul Alastair's boat?" the gentleman asked. He had on cargo shorts and a tan t-shirt with a Wisconsin Badger baseball cap. Red hair curled out under it, matching his fiery red facial hair, his emerald green eyes blazing under the hat. Andrew thought this man had to be at least in his forties and seemed in shape for his age.

"Yes, it is. I'm Andrew Monroe, one of the workers on the boat. Paul will be back soon he had to run to his house for equipment." Andrew stated as he hauled the next plastic lobster trap on the rail.

"My name is Jameson O'Reilly, but everyone calls me James. It's nice to meet you," James said to Andrew as he stuck out his hand for a very firm handshake. Andrew wasn't expecting the strength behind it.

"How do you know Paul?" Andrew asked intrigued. He took his lukewarm water bottle from the dock, taking a long swig.

"We were in Iraq together back in 2009. We stayed friends ever since. I recently moved here after retiring from the military a couple of months ago. Paul said that he would show me around town." James chimed, wiping sweat with his t-shirt sleeve. Andrew didn't notice it at first but now he couldn't help, but think there was something very familiar about this man.

"Might be a weird question, but have we met before? Is this your first time in Maine? Or have you visited before?

Sorry, it just seems like I have seen you somewhere," Andrew asked, feeling somewhat embarrassed.

James cocked his head to the side, studying Andrew. "No, this is my first time here."

The more Andrew talked to James, the more certain he felt he knew James. It was deep down in his gut. He racked his brain on where the hell he saw James before. "Where are you originally from?"

"Wisconsin." James grinned, pointing to his head. "What made you move to Maine, if I may ask? Have any family?" Andrew asked, more intrigued than ever.

"Well after retiring, I didn't really have any other real place to go. My wife divorced me a long time ago. I have a daughter, but I can't find her at all. I have no idea where she could have gone." He stated sadly. Andrew saw James shoulder drop and it was like a cloud casted over the man. It was obvious that he loved his daughter. Andrew's heart went out for the man and prayed that one day he could see her again.

"I am so sorry to hear that. What's your daughter's name? Andrew urged. Andrew could see the pride this man had for his daughter and James seemed to melt at the mention of her.

James grinned, "My Ellie, the last time I saw her she was six." He said sadly, rubbing his hand through his hair then placing his hat back on. Andrew's body was on fire.

"No...Could this be?" Andrew pondered, convinced he saw this man's face before. "Is Ellie her real name or nickname?" Andrew asked, his body bubbling with excitement.

James looked confused, "Her nickname, her actual name is Eleanor."

CHAPTER FOURTEEN

"It couldn't have been a more perfect day," Eleanor thought as she and Amelia walked down Main Street. The breeze coming off the water was nice and crisp. It made the sun's rays seem less daunting as they traveled through downtown Hope Harbor. Eleanor thought this was a perfect way not just to see the town, but hopefully get her and Amelia's mind off the events of the last few days. They passed countless old shops that were beautifully decorated with flowers and banners on the sales they were having. Amelia stopped at the local book store. It had a big panel window, in the front and was painted with a deep, rich, sea blue. It looked old, weathered, and very inviting. Eleanor could see why Amelia was drawn to it. Owl's Nest Books was painted with an elegant, whimsical font on top of the store building with gold tone paint. It had the latest books displayed on shelves looking out at the street.

"Can we go in, Eleanor?!" Amelia asked excitedly, not bothering to wait for the answer. A bell rang as she opened the old wooden door that creaked loudly. They both paused and gasped in awe at the exquisite interior of the antique store. The walls were painted with a deeper blue with wooden rustic shelves from high ceiling to floor, overfilled with books of all sizes. Eleanor knew Amelia would dig into every book she could lay her hands on. She always had a deep love of literature. Eleanor could remember countless hours they would spend having deep discussions on classic books such as *Jane Eyre* or *Pride and Prejudice*.

"You're in heaven, aren't you?" Eleanor chuckled as she watched Amelia with her wide eyes as she frantically scanned the store.

Amelia didn't say anything, but Eleanor knew she didn't have to. Eleanor let Amelia wander the store. The aroma of old books and heavenly sweet smells of vanilla and cinnamon swirled through the air. Any nerves that she might have been feeling faded and her body began to hum with the sweet music that played overhead in the speakers. Eleanor closed her eyes and she heard hypnotic harp and violin, melodies intertwining as the notes seemed to dance and twirl into the night like wind cascading over the waves of the ocean. It sent her across the sea to the breath-taking field of Ireland. Eleanor must find out the album so she could hear more of the calming melody that soothed her weary soul.

Behind the counter was an elderly lady that looked a lot like Elizabeth, Andrew's neighbor. The lady had to be in her late sixties. Her vibrant silver hair with streaks of black was pulled into a braid that was draped across her shoulder. She had high cheek bones and a soft, heart-shaped face. Her sapphire eyes glimmered in the light of the flickering candles she had on the counter. Her eyes met Eleanor's and her smile brightened, smoothing the wrinkles on her cheeks. Eleanor smiled back, enchanted by this quaint store and the regal woman that worked there.

"Hi, I'm Beatrice. Welcome to Owl's Nest. How may

I help you?" she asked sweetly, her words almost a song.

"Hi," Eleanor whispered, hoping that Amelia couldn't hear her. "My cousin just moved here and has a great passion for literature. I was wondering if you have any part-time work available. Amelia is very loyal and trustworthy. She would be in her element here and I believe that she could do amazing things here in Hope Harbor. She just needs a chance," Eleanor stated proudly. Amelia had never let anyone down and Eleanor sensed that she could make this place more magical then it already was.

Beatrice pondered for a moment, eyes squinting as her finger tapped her lower lip. "I would like to meet her first," she stated not looking totally convinced. As if on cue, Amelia appeared around the corner with a stack of books in her hands, flushed with excitement.

"Amelia, this is Beatrice," Eleanor gestured to each one in turn. Eleanor watched Beatrice's facial expression change from uncertain to ecstatic. Her eyes grew wide and she clapped her hands placing them over her heart.

"I have been waiting for you." She shouted, enthusiastically, staring at Amelia. Amelia looked at Eleanor confused then back at Beatrice.

"For me, why?" Amelia asked confused and a little scared.

"You're hired, Amelia. You start tomorrow. I have plans for you my dear. Great, amazing plans," she sang. She started humming as she wrote down something on a piece of paper. Eleanor and Amelia just looked at each other dumbfounded, but Eleanor could see the excitement in Amelia's eyes. "When you come in tomorrow, I will get down all your information. I open at eight, so please be here by then. We are open till four tomorrow so if you can stay the whole day that would be great. I am greatly looking forward to working with you. You're exactly what this book store needs," Beatrice said, grinning.

Eleanor saw Amelia let out a big sigh, looking like she was on cloud nine. "Thank you so much Beatrice! I will see you tomorrow," She smiled. Amelia paid for her books and they quickly walked out. Once they got outside Eleanor and Amelia looked at each other than both started shrieking, jumping up and down in excitement.

"Excuse me... are you ladies okay?" a voice boomed, making both of them jump in shock. They both turned to see a very handsome man in a Hope Harbor police uniform. He had the clearest ivory skin and a rounded baby face with sharp cheek bones. His crimson red hair curled upward under his police hat, matching the color of his facial hair. His sky blue eyes blazed as he smirked at the two of them. Eleanor saw him glance at Amelia and his pupils widened.

"Yes, sorry we just got excited," Eleanor chuckled. As she continued to gaze at him, she felt like he looked familiar.

"It's okay, Eleanor," he grinned as he shifted the box of donuts under one arm, so he could extend his hand toward her. "I'm David."

"Nice to meet you, David," Eleanor said, smiling slightly, confused at how he knew her name. She slowly took his hand. She seemed to be improving on her interaction with men. He next shook Amelia's hand, both of their faces blushing.

"I am Ryan's brother, the good looking one," he chuckled. "You're coming to our barbeque tomorrow, right? Surely Andrew has told you about it?!" he asked as he took a quick glance at Amelia. Too bad, that couldn't have been more obvious.

"Actually he hasn't. I haven't seen him today," Eleanor stated sadly.

David must of seen it in her eyes, "Well...he probably was going to tell you today Eleanor. You both are very welcome to come. It's at five," he said grabbing a napkin out of his box, writing down his address to his dad's house. "I will see both of you there!" he said, glancing once more at Amelia.

"Sounds good...thank you. We will see you tomorrow!" Eleanor chimed in, trying to break that poor boy's trance over her cousin. Amelia blushed then nodded. David tipped his hats at them and then went on his way. When David was out of sight, the girls turned to each other and giggled wildly. "That poor boy, did you see what you did to him?" Eleanor laughed.

"I have no idea what you're talking about!" Amelia chuckled.

Eleanor could only shake her head. "Oh if you only knew." Eleanor thought to herself.

Andrew sped through town, passing David Alastair as he sat in his squad car parked in the local gas station. They made eye contact, David rolling his eyes and shaking his head. Andrew yelled out the window. "Sorry!"

He quickly parked in her driveway and ran up to the door, pounding harder than he intended to. Amelia opened up the door and Andrew strode right in, not even asking for permission.

"Andrew, is something wrong?" Eleanor asked

frantically running up to him, searching over his body as if he were wounded.

Andrew, who didn't realize he was panting, let out a huge sigh as he stared firmly at Eleanor, "I need to ask you a very important question," he said, pensive as he placed both hands on each side of her shoulders. Her eyes widened and her mouth parted a little, her rich copper hair looked windblown around her. He had never seen anything more delectable.

"What are you doing tomorrow?" Andrew asked trying to regain focus.

Her eye brows furrowed. "Tomorrow? Amelia and I have a party to go to. We got invited by this really nice guy we met today," she smiled, making a sly glance at Amelia.

He squinted his eyes at her. "Who was this man? Someone I would know?" he asked, becoming more suspicious by the minute.

Amelia chimed in then, "Oh, he was extremely handsome and looks really good in uniform...pretty sure he has the hots for Eleanor!" Amelia giggled, Eleanor giggling with her, only making Andrew rolled his eyes.

"You both will be the death of me!!" He shouted.

"David that big flirt, I told him..." Andrew stopped, before he put his foot in his mouth.

"He wasn't flirting with me, but he was with Amelia!" She said, reassuring Andrew. "So why is it so important that we go tomorrow?" Eleanor asked, intrigued as she headed into the kitchen to start supper. Andrew and Amelia followed her into the kitchen, sitting at either ends of the table.

"I just thought it would be a good way to meet more people from town," Andrew lied. He could feel Amelia's stare from across the table. He turned to look at her and she knew that he was lying. Amelia's eyebrow rose as she had the expression on her face saying,

"You better tell me what you're hiding," he didn't say anything to Amelia, but with Eleanor's back turned to them he nodded, in agreement to their silent conversation.

Andrew was on his way to his truck when Amelia stopped at his truck.

"I know your hiding something from Eleanor. I don't like it. I know we don't know each other that well, but I know you're in love with her," she paused, as Andrew's eyes widened and his cheeks flushed. He was about to open his mouth to deny it, but she held up her hand to stop him. "No, don't say you don't. Everyone can tell, well except for her," she paused becoming angry at him. "So spill it or we aren't going tomorrow," she demanded.

Andrew was shocked at how she stood up to him. He knew he was intimidating to many, but it was refreshing that Amelia couldn't care less about Andrew's size. He let out a sigh and then told Amelia of his meeting of who he believed was Eleanor's father.

"You're positive it's him?" Amelia asked, unconvinced.

"Yes, Amelia. You have to believe me. I wouldn't do this as some cruel trick. She needs her father and I know he needs her. Can you please make sure she gets there?" he said pleading with her. She scrunched her lips to one side, with a questionable look on her face. He was hanging on by a thread.

"If it's not him and you break her heart, so help me I will break your face," she said, bluntly. Andrew grabbed Amelia's hand and squeezed.

"You have my word. I promise. That is the last thing I would ever do," he promised her. She squeezed his hand back, nodding. She dropped it and walked back into the house without looking back. He knew bringing up the past would be a major risk, but that was a risk he was willing to take.

CHAPTER FIFTHTEEN

"What is taking you so long in there? It's almost been an hour and we will be late!" Rachel shouted from the other side of the bathroom door. Eleanor spent half the time in the bathroom fidgeting and moving and adjusting her clothes, which took her almost half the morning to pick out. She felt that this was a big moment for her and Andrew. They were finally going out in public as a couple. She was terrified with this being her first relationship, her first boyfriend. She had a lot riding on this and she wanted it to be perfect. Right now, however, she was more worried about people seeing her scars. It was a nice warm, slightly humid day, but she was stuck wearing a three quarters long shirt and faded capris. She'd lain awake the night before, sleepless with thoughts of others in town finding out about her secret.

"Eleanor, honey, it will be okay, I promise. Please open up," Rachel said in a softer voice. Eleanor stared at herself in the mirror, letting out a sigh in defeat. Slowly opening the door, Rachel and Amelia stood on the other side with both of their arms open. Eleanor's heart burst and she rushed into their arms. It felt so good to have such warmth and love surround her once again. She didn't have to hide and be afraid. They knew her secret and supported and nourished her into being a better person. She tried to hold back the tears as both of them caressed her back. They pulled her back and gave her a once over.

"You look beautiful honey. We promise." Amelia smiled, glancing at Rachel who nodded in agreement. Eleanor blushed, glancing in the mirror one more time.

"Girl, your turn is done! I got to look hot for any single men!" Rachel laughed out, rushing past Eleanor in the bathroom glancing closely at the mirror. Amelia and Eleanor looked at each other and laughed.

"This day should be interesting." Amelia mumbled giggling as they walked into the living room.

"I heard that!" Rachel shouted, Eleanor and Amelia bursting out in giggles once more. It felt good to laugh.

Eleanor and her friends were in awe of the extravagant house that stood before them on top of the hill on Grace Court, overlooking Pearl Bay. The gray two-story cottage had white window trim and a bright blue door, standing tall and proud at the edge of a cliff while overlooking the water below. Eleanor could feel the electricity from the house and the sea below.

Rachel and Amelia went ahead of Eleanor, which she didn't mind. She was taking in all she could. She followed the others toward the back of the house. The south end of the house had top to bottom windows. Eleanor could just picture herself sitting in a chair in front of the windows with a good book as she watched the waves crash upon the rocks.

"Eleanor!" a man's voice shouted, breaking her daydream. She turned to see Ryan walking towards her with a smile that could melt any woman's heart.

"Hi, Ryan, this place is amazing! I can't believe you grew up here." Eleanor smiled. Ryan chuckled as he stopped in front of her, his eyes crinkling from smiling. She couldn't deny that he was a beautiful man.

"My mom will love to hear what you think of it. She takes great pride in maintaining it. This was her dream home. It didn't always look like this, but throughout the years my mom did an amazing job bringing out the beauty in this majestic house. I will definitely have you meet her."

"I would like that a lot! Have you seen Andrew?" Eleanor asked graciously, glancing around.

"Yes, he is out back with my dad and Trevor. Did you bring any guests with you? David said that your cousin is living with you now," Ryan asked.

"Yes I brought Amelia-my cousin, and my friend Rachel."

"That's nice. I hope they both have fun. You will have to introduce me to them," he said. Eleanor and Ryan chatted a little more as slowly made their way toward the back of the house.

Eleanor gasped when she noticed how gorgeous the view was from the cliff. It took her breath away, goosebumps crawled over her body. She loved those moments when nature showed its spectacular beauty. She glanced across the yard to see another beauty, Andrew. She still couldn't believe that he had feelings for her, damage included. He saw right through into her soul. He understood her better than she understood herself at times. Andrew peered up and met her eyes as if he knew she was thinking of him. A big smile crossed his face, showing the dimples on his clean shaven face. Heat rose up her face, and her lungs got tight. It still felt like the first time she met him and she hoped that feeling would never go away. He motioned to Trevor and they both started making their way to her. Trevor ran to her, meeting her first, embracing her in a big hug. Trevor knew how to melt Eleanor. He pulled away with the biggest smile on his face.

"Hey, buddy! I have missed you!" Eleanor smiled, hugging him again. Trevor didn't say anything. They had a connection where they didn't need to talk to communicate. They just seemed to know what the other person was thinking or feeling.

"Okay, my turn bud!" Andrew chuckled as he wrapped his muscular arms around Eleanor. She sighed as they molded together as one. He gave off such security it was like a warm blanket on a cold winter night. He picked her up and swung her around, both of them laughing. As he put her down, he gently kissed the tip of her nose. If he wasn't holding her up at that time, she would have dissolved into the ground. "I've missed you," he whispered, roughly.

Eleanor couldn't help but giggle. "I missed you too," as she stared into his ocean blue eyes, everyone just seemed to fade away until it was just them. She knew he felt it too. She brought her hand up to his cheek and caressed it lightly. He closed his eyes taking in her touch. She wanted to live in this moment forever.

As the evening carried on, the sun slowly began to set on the horizon casting a wonderful array of deep purples, reds, pinks, and blues. This was Eleanor's favorite part of the day. Eleanor remembered when she and Claire would sit on the deck with a drink and soft music playing. The birds seemed to harmonize with the melody of the song and the fireflies would dance to the beat. They would sit in silence watching the world turn to night. The breeze would dance on their skin and play with their hair. It seemed as if time stood still. Eleanor would give anything to just have one more sunset with Claire.

Andrew broke her from her trance when he entwined his fingers with hers. She shook her thoughts away. "Follow me, I want you to meet someone," he said, pulling her along through the yard. He led the way down the hill. It seemed like they were walking forever until they stopped.

She looked around but was confused. Andrew tapped his finger on some strangers shoulder having him turn around to face them. She glanced at Andrew who was smiling, even though his gaze was directed to the person in front of them. Eleanor peered at the stranger, blind-sided by the only man she would never have expected to ever see again.

"Is this a joke?" she said in disbelief, as she stared in front of a bright, ginger-haired man that had her same eyes, her mouth and nose, Jameson O'Reilly...her father. She would never forget that face. He looked much older than she remembered, but she could recognize those blue-green eyes anywhere.

"Ellie, oh my...is that really you?" he cried, reaching out for her, tear's rolling down his cheeks. She held up her hand and backed away. Never in a million years would she believe that she would be standing in front of her father again. He died; she remembered that day perfectly. All the questions that she had ever wanted to ask him rushed through her mind, but she wasn't able to produce the words. She didn't know what to feel, until rage started pumping through her veins. He was alive all this time, but why didn't he tell her? Why couldn't he have come for her? He could have saved her from Dan.

"No...no, this can't be true," she whimpered,

backing up more. She felt as if the world was crushing down on her.

"You died... mother told me you died in Iraq. I mourned for you all these years and yet you were alive the whole time," she paused, her throat becoming constricted. "You never once sent me any letters saying that you were alive. How could you do that to me?" she stopped herself.

Jameson's eyebrows furrowed together. "Eleanor, your mother divorced me. She told me I could never see you again and got primary custody over you. I had no choice being overseas. I sent you a letter and a gift every month for a year, but I never received any word from you. I figured you were mad at me or that your mother said something to make you not want to talk to me. I had no idea what she told you. I can't even imagine..."he trailed off, wiping his cheek from the stream of tears.

Eleanor had never seen her dad emotional when she was younger. For a moment she wanted to run up to him and hug him. Forget everything that happened in the past. She was torn; crying because she was happy that her father was alive and angry as hell at her mother for lying to her for all those years. She never thought her mother could have stooped so low, this was even before her mother met Dan. Her anger for her father slowly diminished. Eleanor started to cry as her once shattered wall slowly began to build around her. She could sense the air stiffen and thicken with suffocating heat; smoke swirling all around her. She glanced at Andrew.

He didn't take his eyes off her and he too became stiff, his jaw clenching. "Don't Eleanor, I know what you're doing. Please don't do this to your father. He doesn't know. He won't hurt you!" he consoled her in a soft voice. Jameson looked at Andrew confused and then back at Eleanor.

"It's not that simple..." she whimpered, as she stared at her father. "I'm not the Ellie you used to know."

She turned to run as fast as her legs could take her, in any direction but there. She heard someone yell. "Don't!" It sounded like Amelia; she knew that Amelia wouldn't let anyone come after her.

Eleanor ran where the wind took her, her vision becoming blurrier by the second. She collapsed a mile down the beach that she miraculously found. She fell to her knees causing pin needle pain to shoot through her skin as she hit the sand with force. She let out a sorrowful sob, clutching her head in her hands and praying to God that this wasn't happening. It was happening all too fast and she just couldn't handle one more chip on her shoulder. She cried till her chest hurt and her eyes burned and she had no voice left. Her body felt weak and her mind slowly faded in and out. Night began to set in, darkness surrounded her and for the first time in a long time, she welcomed it.

CHAPTER SIXTEEN

Andrew watched as Eleanor fled the down the hill into the woods. His blood pounded through his body and he started off after her, but Amelia stepped into the way. His impatience was getting the best of him.

"Don't! I don't think she wants to see anyone right now. Just let her be. She needs some space," Amelia tried to reassure Andrew. He thought of just picking up Amelia, setting her to the side and running like hell after Eleanor, but deep down he knew that she was right. Eleanor needed space, he felt that maybe he should have forewarned her, but would she have come if she knew? Andrew knew the answer and that is why he didn't say anything. He had no idea that she would take such happy news like this and twist it, but he didn't know the entire story. It still put him on edge, the way she left.

"What if she gets hurt?" he asked frantically, as he began to pace back and forth, running his hand through his hair.

"You have to give her more credit, Andrew. She is a smart girl, but right now I think seeing anyone is the last thing she wants. She stated, looking at Andrew then

Jameson. Jameson was on the ground, knees to his chest with his head into hands. Andrew couldn't tell if he was crying or not. "I will head home to see if she ended up there. I will call you and let you know," she assured him. She put her hands on Andrew's and Jameson shoulders. They both looked up at her. She nodded. "It will be okay. Uncle James...it's good to have you back," she smiled slightly, bending down to give him a hug. Andrew could see it took all of Jameson's effort not to break down right then. Ryan in handed both Andrew and Jameson a cold beer. Andrew sat next to Jameson in the cold damp grass. They sat in silence looking toward the direction Eleanor ran off too. Andrew wasn't sure what exactly to say, he couldn't imagine what was going through Jameson's head. Andrew stared out into the distance, hoping and praying that Eleanor would come back through the tall grass and everything would be okay.

Jameson suddenly turned toward Andrew. "How do you know Eleanor?"

Andrew couldn't help but smirk. Andrew relayed the story of how they first met when he called to talk to Claire, and then again when she moved to Maine. He added. "I was so mad at her the first time I actually met her in person. At the time I didn't know it was her."

"Why were you mad at her?" Jameson asked, concerned.

He couldn't help but chuckle as he relayed the story of his first meeting with Eleanor and the significance of her relationship with his brother Trevor. "I have never seen two people have such a deeper bond before. I am happy they have each other," Andrew said, smiling to himself. He turned to Jameson who was staring at him.

"So is that when you fell for her?" Jameson asked, in a serious tone.

Andrew leaned back, his face starting to blush. He coughed and shook his head, trying to decide if he heard Jameson right or not. "I'm not in lov…" Andrew began to say.

"Young man, I know when a man is in love. I have been there before," Jameson said in all sincerity.

Andrew chuckled embarrassed. He felt like Jameson could read him like a book. "Am I that obvious?" Andrew asked sighing, his head dropping between his legs.

"You know, love has a tendency of blooming when you least expect it. I have a feeling that you need her as much as she needs you… and don't tell me I'm wrong boy, cause you got it smeared all over your face," Jameson said truthfully.

They sat back in silence once more, but for Andrew it was more comfortable than before. That feeling soon changed when he saw Amelia run up the hill toward them, her face tormented. Andrew's heart jumped up into his chest. He and Jameson both jumped up and rushed toward Amelia. "I can't find her. She didn't show up and I have been looking for her," she cried.

Ryan rushed to Andrew's side, along with Rachel. All five of them headed out in the direction that Eleanor went too. There was a trail at the bottom of the hill. It was laden with wildflowers on both sides and rock fragments. Jameson, Andrew, and Amelia headed off in one direction with Ryan and Rachel heading off in the opposite. Andrew's heart pounded loudly in his chest and he ran as fast has his legs would take him. They soon reached a clearing that led to a small beach. The sun was sinking faster into the sky and the light was becoming limited.

"Eleanor!!" Andrew shouted at the top of his voice.

He started running in the direction of some large granite rocks. His mind was going a mile a minute. Once he passed the first huge rock, he stopped dead in his tracks. On the ground a few yards away from him, he saw the end of her hair lying on top of the sand.

"Oh god!" he thought. He rushed to her side to see her huddled in a fetal position. He couldn't see her face beneath the strands of hair. He knelt down beside her, gently pushing the hair out of her face. She stirred a little but then stopped. Once he got all the hair out of her face, he realized that she was sleeping. He could see the tear stains and her puffy eyes and knew she cried herself to sleep.

"Over here!!" he shouted. He slowly bent down, kissing her cheek. "Eleanor, I'm here honey," he whispered in her ear, but she didn't wake up or make a sound. Jameson reached where they were located and helped Andrew lift her up from the tight corner that she was positioned in. They got back to the house where Ryan and Rachel were waiting.

"She was sleeping down by the rocks. The tide almost got her," Jameson said speaking softly. Andrew felt how cold Eleanor was. She began to shiver against his chest.

"She needs to get home, she feels like ice," Andrew said, heading toward her car.

"Amelia, if you don't mind I would like to meet you at the house and spend the night to make sure she is okay," he asked Amelia, nodded as she grabbed her and Eleanor's things. "Ryan, could you watch Trevor for the night, please?"

"You got it bud," he said morosely.

"Are you okay, man?" Andrew asked quietly. Andrew noticed Ryan glance at Rachel then back at him.

Smiling weakly, Ryan said. "Yeah man, just get her home."

"I'm coming with you," Jameson stated, grabbing his stuff.

Andrew shook his head, "Not tonight. Please, I don't know if it's best right now. Just let her get some sleep and maybe in the morning. We'll see if she is willing to see you," Jameson sighed in defeat.

"I will be there in the morning whether you like it or not," he said sternly.

Andrew didn't want to start a fight with her father. He just nodded then headed toward Eleanor's vehicle, carefully placing her in the backseat of the car. He jogged to his truck and followed Amelia back to the house. His mind was flying through the possible outcomes of the past hour, each one more tragic than the other. He felt that she just couldn't seem to win. One moment something good was happening then she gets struck down, but with her dad being here, in the same town, around the same time as Eleanor, has to be a sign. The only thing now is trying to convince Eleanor.

Eleanor awoke to soft blankets and a down pillow. She blinked her eyes a couple times to realize that she was back in her room, in her bed. The curtains were closed except for a small slit that leaked morning light. She lay there for a while just focusing on the light until she realized that someone was in the room with her. In the corner by her closet sitting in the dark was a figure. A chill rose over Eleanor as she sat up frightened, covering herself up with the blanket.

"I'm sorry sweetie, I didn't mean to scare you." her dad said softly. Her body surprisingly calm to his tone.

"What are you doing here?" she asked, trying to keep her voice steady.

"After Amelia realized you didn't come home last night, Amelia, Andrew, and I with some others went to find you. I'm glad we found you when we did because the tide was starting to rise and you could have been swept away," he choked out. "Andrew was very adamant about me not seeing you, but I have lost you before, I am not willing to lose you again," Eleanor coughed, trying to hold back the tears that suddenly appeared.

"I am sorry about yesterday. I overreacted..." she cried, trailing off.

Jameson picked up his chair and dragged it closer to the bed. Once he passed the light, she could see how worn out he had been and it was all her fault.

"You didn't know, honey, you had no idea. Like you said you thought I was dead," he paused. "How could she do that to you? Telling you I died," he choked out his words.

Eleanor sighed deeply. She was torn that her mother not only hurt her, but hurt her father. She didn't feel so alone in that moment. "Well she did a lot of things..." she said, stopping. Her father sat up straighter in the chair. He put his hand on his inner thigh, as if trying to hold himself up with his arm.

"Eleanor, what things...Is there something you're not telling me, with those scars?" he paused, Eleanor heard him gulp. "How many do you have?"

Eleanor sat there in silence, broken. She wanted to have her dad in her life. They missed out on so much together, it wouldn't be bad to start making up for lost time. For Eleanor to open up to one of most the important people in her life would be more of a struggle than she realized. She was apprehensive about opening her heart to someone so significant only to have a chance of losing them. She took the deepest breath she could and told her father the story of her traumatic childhood.

He huffed, trying to hold back his pain. "Do you only have them on your arms?"

Her body sagged lower into the bed, "No..." she paused. "On both arms, back, and legs. Dad...I," she cried. She felt him sitting on the bed next to her and then felt him wrap his massive arms around her. She leaned into him, her head on his chest.

He began to rock her, cooing her. "Shh...It's okay Ellie. You don't have to tell me anymore now. I am not going anywhere my love. I will never leave you again," he paused pulling back and cradling her head into his hands, making her look up at him. "I am going to make up for not being there. I love you, my Ellie."

She opened her mouth to say the words back but she stopped. She knew she loved her father but saying those three words, petrified her. She closes her mouth and looked at him in dismay. He smiles warmly at her, "Ellie, I know you love me, it's okay," he reassured her as he wraps her in a hug. Her body automatically tensed for a split second but then relaxed as her father gently kissed the top of her head while rocking her. She never wanted to leave this moment. Never in her wildest dreams would her father be here, accepting her scars and all. She knew from this day, a new beginning was rising, but there was still a darkness drifting over the horizon.

CHAPTER SEVENTEEN

Eleanor woke up with a huge smile on her face as she lay on her grandmother's comforter, listening to the birds singing outside her window. Her hair fanned out around her as she ran her fingers through the tousled curls. Eleanor couldn't contain her excitement about what was ahead for the day. She planned a small gathering at her house to thank her family and friends for being there for her in her time of need.

She had a lot of duties to perform before people arrived. With Amelia at the bookstore, she didn't know how long it would take her to finish. Andrew texted her the night before saying he would be over earlier to help and her father insisted on coming in the morning as well. She couldn't think of two better people she would rather be with right now.

She sprang out of bed, grabbing a quick cup of coffee for fuel as she headed outside. There was a little chill to the air, so she grabbed a light jacket and put it on before turning the lawn mower on to cut what seemed to be an endless yard. Part of her was wondering why she bought a small cottage with such a huge lawn. She could only laugh because she knew without a doubt that she was in love with this cottage the moment she saw it. She stuck in ear buds to drown out the noise and soon was lost in her thoughts as she started the motor.

A vehicle pulled into the drive, but it wasn't Andrew's or anyone that she knew. She turned off the mower and started walking toward them. A man and woman got out of the car. The woman had shoulder length hair that was brown like hers. Eleanor's body froze and blood drained to her feet making her stop where she was.

"Hello my Eleanor..." she exclaimed, running up to her and giving her a hug. Eleanor couldn't move or breathe.

"M-mom...what are you doing here?" she choked out. "I missed you, darlin', why else would I be here?" She said, playfully slapped her arm, making Eleanor stiffen. Abigail seemed to age dramatically, her skin sagging around her chin and wrinkles along her eyes and mouth.

"What do you want?" Eleanor snapped, hating that familiar feeling that started to gnaw at her, fear.

"That is no way to talk to your mother!" Dan yelled, stepping forward. The face Eleanor remembered all too well, the face that would laugh when she would scream as he would burn her with his cigarette or worse. She took a step back, frozen in fear, which made him chuckle. "You remember me then don't you...all the fun times we used to have, Ellie?" he paused raising an eyebrow, "You want to play our favorite game?"

"Where is the money, you little brat?!" Abigail interrupted him, taking a step closer to Eleanor. "Where is my money?!"

Fury consumed her. "That money is not yours and

never will be! Is that all your family can think of? Did you not care that your own mother died?" she snapped, taking a step forward, clenching her fist tightly.

Abigail laughed. "I don't have to answer any of your questions. You think you're so brave standing up to us..." she grinned, turning to her boyfriend. "Why don't you two play and then maybe you will tell us where it is then." She said grinning and clapping her hands together.

"You both can go to hell!" Eleanor shouted, swinging her hand toward Abigail, slapping her across the face. Pushing her to the ground, she shouted. "Now you know how it feels to be beaten. You were never there for me!!" she screamed, sending another slap.

Abigail's boyfriend charged at Eleanor, pulling her off of her mother and threw her onto the ground, swinging his fist and hitting her hard in the face. Feeling a crunch, pain shot through her face as she cradled it in her hands. He gave Eleanor another blow this time with his foot kicking her hard twice in the ribs. She let out a blood curdling scream hoping someone would hear her.

"No one is going to save you this time..." he chided as he stomped down on her left leg. Eleanor felt the snap of a bone breaking as a surge of immense pain consumed her. He bent down over the top of her as he continued to unleash punch after punch. She held her arms up to deflect his blows, but it seemed useless. Her strength was diminishing fast and blackness was beginning to consume her.

The ground started to vibrate as another car pulled into the driveway. Eleanor heard a commotion as whoever got out started yelling and then, grunts and sounds of a struggle. There was no way she could have moved. She felt as if there was a rock on top of her and she could feel herself begin to go in and out of consciousness.

Then as if an angel was directing her home, she heard that familiar voice, "Eleanor..."

Andrew was lucky that Ryan came with him when he did, because otherwise Andrew would have killed that man right then and there. He would never forget that image of that man on top of Eleanor, throwing punches as her body lay motionless on the ground. For a heart breaking moment, Andrew's thought his worst nightmare had come true.

Andrew and Ryan both barged out onto the lawn, rushing to Eleanor as Ryan pulled the man off of Eleanor and held him down while Andrew peered over Eleanor's bloody and swollen body. He checked her vitals, her pulse was slow and her breathing ragged. He called 911. His heart raged with hate as he turned to see the couple staring at him. The woman stood there with a blank look on her face. Her cheekbones and lips reminded him of Eleanor; he knew then that was her mother. He noticed that the left side of her face was pink and her bottom lip was bleeding. He felt small pride knowing that Eleanor probably gave that to her.

"How could you do this to your own daughter?" he bellowed, charging at her. She took a few steps back. The man started to struggle in Ryan's grasp as Andrew approached her. He turned to the man. "I will deal with you soon enough."

She backed up into a tree and looked scared out of her mind, her lower lip quivering. "Don't pull this sad crap on me, you bitch!" he snapped, punching the tree right next to her head. Pain shot up his arm, but he didn't care.

She gasped and began to cry. "I just wanted my money, and she didn't deserve it." she cried.

"She deserves that and a hell of a lot more than you. All the shit you put her through. All I can say to you, is karma is a bitch!" he shouted, getting mere inches from her face. He turned his head to the man who had a big smirk on his face. Andrew smirked back at him, raising an eyebrow. "You want to see something funny, watch this," as he swung back his arm and punched the guy as hard as he could in the face.

The man groaned out in pain and he fell on his knees. Blood poured out his nose.

Ryan looked up at Andrew with a concerned expression. "That's enough, man. Please don't get sent to jail with them. She needs you," he gestured toward Eleanor. Andrew turned back to Eleanor's body. Ryan was right. Andrew walked back over to her and got down on his knees to stroke her hair. A lump formed in his chest and he fought the urge to cry. He couldn't imagine if he didn't get there soon enough. He wouldn't know what to do if he lost her. An ache burrowed in his heart and his body felt numb. He quickly tried to bury that thought away.

"Eleanor, please be okay..."he paused trying to hold back the tears.

Jameson showed up right as the ambulance and police did. Jameson rushed to Andrew's side when he noticed him holding Eleanor. Andrew watched as Jameson's eyes fiercely turned into fire. He shot up looking for the culprits; shocked as hell when he realized it was his ex-wife and her boyfriend.

"You!! What in God's name are you doing here?" Abigail hissed, lunging forward toward Jameson, the cop holding her back.

"Being here for my daughter! How dare you treat her like that! You told her I was dead. DEAD! How can you be so selfish?!" Jameson bellowed.

"And you! You made those marks on my daughter!!" Jameson seethed, glancing at Dan who was standing next to Abigail. He threw one punch at Dan dropping him to his knees hard again, blood pouring out of his nose once more.

David, the deputy of Hope Harbor, saw the whole thing as he rushed up to Jameson. "Back away James, it's not worth it. They will get what is coming to them," Andrew watched as Jameson dropped his head, wiping his face with his hand. He glanced back at Andrew who helped Eleanor be escorted into the ambulance by a stretcher. Their eyes met and Jameson strode toward Andrew, grasping him in a hug.

They pulled away looking at each other. David walked up to them, looking to both sides making sure no one was around. "I wanted to tell you both, between us... this is as far as it goes. I found from the report just now that those two have a warrant out in three other states for drug possession, assault and battery. I found reports speculating child abuse but that man over there, Dan Times was never charged," he whispered, looking meaningfully into both of their eyes.

A fire raged through Andrew's veins and his fists drew tighter together, and he snarled, turning to that man. His blood boiled imagining Eleanor as a child and that man doing what he did to her today. Every muscle, nerve, and bone in Andrew's body wanted that man to pay for what he did. Andrew turned and started to charge toward the cop car where Dan was held, but Jameson stopped him right before Andrew could get to him.

"This will not help the situation, Andrew." Jameson shouted, pushing Andrew back. "Think of Eleanor, please. Go to her. She needs us more than ever! Now go!" he declared, pushing Andrew back with a big shove. Andrew stood there motionless when he got to the truck.

Ryan came up behind him, placing his hand on Andrew's shoulder. Andrew looked at Ryan with rage burning in his eyes. "I will get Trevor from group and have him stay at my parents tonight. Call me with any updates. I will stop by the store and let Amelia know what happened. Andrew- Eleanor will be okay. I promise," Ryan stated, trying to reassure him.

Andrew didn't know what to say, he just nodded and wrapped Ryan into a hug. Ryan had always been there for Andrew no matter what. "Thank you for everything," Andrew mumbled.

Ryan's sighed, tightening the hug, "You're welcome bud, now go see your girl and keep me updated." He pulled back nodding. Ryan went to the other side of car, speaking low to Jameson and letting himself be pulled into a hug as well.

On the way to the hospital it was an eerie silence. Andrew kept replaying the image of Eleanor on the ground. A fire raged in the pit of his stomach again and he felt as if he was going to be sick. Images of her brittle body lying in a contorted position, one eye swollen shut, nose broken, and blood smeared all over of her face. Her cheek on the other side gashed open. He wondered just how long that bastard was beating her for. Andrew only knew one thing, he loved Eleanor. He loved her with

every fiber in his body and would do everything in his
power to make sure that bastard paid for what he did...
even if Andrew did it himself.

CHAPTER EIGHTEEN

Eleanor woke to gentle hands and a symphony of voices and sounds. She grimaced once the pain hit her. It was as if someone tore her body limb from limb. Every muscle ached and her head pounded loudly. She opened one eye slightly only seeing shadows of people, the light blinding. She shut her eyes tight welcoming the darkness. The light made her headache worse. She tried to sigh, but abruptly stopped when she got shooting pain across her chest that made her whimper. Even breathing was a battle of constant pain and she just wished she could just be put out of her misery.

Someone must have heard her whimper because the voice of the hand holding hers began to talk. "Eleanor?" the deep voice asked as he caressed her hand. She gave it a light squeeze making the voice gasp and shout for the doctor. "Where's the doctor? She's awake!" he shouted with concern, but relief in his tone. She winced again with the loudness of his voice. "Sorry sweetie." he whispered, stroking her hair.

She knew it was Andrew and wished she could open her eyes to see him.

"Andrew..." she mumbled, whimpering as she realized her lips were swollen. "How bad is it?"

"Shh...you don't need to talk sweetie, I am right here. Your dad is here too, he went to get us some coffee," he said his voice exhausted.

It killed her that she couldn't see his smooth skin, sharp high cheekbones, and stone washed blue eyes. She sighed, pain shooting across her chest. She opened her eye a little at a time, getting adjusted to the light. She started to freak when her other eye wouldn't open. The monitors beeped fast as her pulse started to race. "Why can't I open my other eye?" She thought, frantically looking around the room scared. Her breathing started to quicken causing her pain with every inhale.

"Eleanor, what is wrong honey? Please calm down, everything is okay," he insisted, growing more concerned when Eleanor's breathing became ragged. "Doctor, I think she is having a panic attack," he yelled.

Eleanor couldn't stop her breathing now and the pain crossed her chest became stronger and stronger to the point where she started to cry out in pain.

"Doctor, do something!" Andrew shouted, angrily.

Eleanor prayed desperately for some relief soon. She thought about how death would be so much more peaceful than this. However after the medicine reached her arm, she began to relax. Her breathing became normal and she felt all warm and fuzzy inside. The pain that crashed into her, ceased immediately. She didn't care what it was as long as they didn't stop giving it to her. The doctor stood at the end of her bed reading her chart. Through Eleanor's swollen eyes she could make out he was an older man, with dark skin.

"Hello Eleanor. My name is Dr. Brutus and I will be your doctor. If you need anything just hit that button that is attached to your hand. Your injuries are quite extensive and I will be preparing surgery for you this afternoon..." he stated, but Eleanor stopped listening.

"Surgery?" she glanced over at Andrew who was listening to the doctor. His face seemed to age ten years over night. Bags formed under his eyes, age lines appeared on his forehead and his skin looked rough. His beard seemed to have grown from a five o'clock shadow when she last saw him to a nice, full on beard.

She turned back to the doctor who didn't stop talking. "Your leg needs to be re-broken and set back in the proper place," he reassured nodding. "We will have you up and ready for the operating room within the hour," he told her, placing her chart back on the clip at the end of the bed before leaving the room. She just watched him walk away like it wasn't a big deal. Her heart sunk deeper in her chest. She hoped he would walk back in the room and just say he was joking. She could feel Andrew's gaze on her and for some reason she was too nervous to look at him.

"Eleanor, please look at me," he whispered as if he read her mind. A tear rolled down her cheek as she slowly turned toward him. She will never forget that look of anguish on his face.

"Eleanor, please don't cry..." he said, getting up from his chair and sitting gently next to her on the bed. He wrapped his arms around her lightly making sure he wouldn't hurt her. "It will be okay Ellie, I'm here," he whispered in her ear.

"No, you're going to leave me," she mumbled hoarsely, her throat burning, sobbing more into his shoulder.

"Shh...no honey, I promise now and forever to be by your side. Eleanor, I..." he paused, lightly turning her face toward his. He peered deep into her eyes. He ever so gently kissed her swollen shut eye, then her broken nose, and then her cheek. "I love you," he declared, staring into her soul and heart. She felt the words in her bones and became numb for a moment. Emotions flowed over her like a waterfall, entrenched in her pores, sinking deep in every fiber of her muscles and grain of her bones. Her eyes grew heavy as she continued to look at him speechless. She wanted to believe it was true, but she felt this moment must be a dream. The overwhelming urge to sleep consumed her and she slowly sank into the pillow as her mind played images of Andrew. "I love you Andrew..." she mumbled, falling into a deep sleep.

Andrew left the room while Eleanor slept peacefully and pain free for the first time in days. He felt as if he was flying when she told him that she loved him. He actually didn't expect her to say anything back. He thought she would argue with him and tell him that he couldn't or she wasn't good enough for him like the times she doubted herself before. He wanted to prove to her more than ever that she was all he ever wanted. She brought him up from the darkness. Now it was his time to bring her out of the darkness and this time for good. He walked down to the café to meet Jameson and instead ran into Rachel and Amelia.

"Hi Andrew, how is she?" Amelia asked, eyes puffy from crying.

He nodded, relaying the message that him and Eleanor received minutes ago. His voice trailed off as his emotion got the best of him as he saw the expressions that crossed Amelia's and Rachel's face. "She looks horrible, almost unrecognizable..." he cried, his will breaking as tears flow down his face. They both embraced him in a tight hug, crying together.

Someone coughed and Andrew turned to see Jameson sitting at the table. They all joined him as he handed each of them a cup of coffee. In the middle of the table was a bouquet of white lilies and roses. Andrew smiled slightly knowing that those were Eleanor's favorite flowers. He relayed the same message to Jameson as he did the girls. Over the next couple hours, they made arrangements on staying and helping with Eleanor once she got back home.

"Hey sweetie, can I come in?" Eleanor's dad asked, as he opened the door slowly. Eleanor nodded, squirming slightly trying to get comfortable, but there was no use. He looked at her injuries and she could see tears well up in his eyes. It pained her to see her father cry.

"Dad, please don't cry. I'm okay," she said, reassuring not just him, but herself.

He took the seat next to her, setting the bouquet of flowers on the dresser beside the bed. She turned her head the best she could to see them. The room erupted with a heavenly floral smell and it brought her back to being with Claire as she worked at the floral shop. The smell calmed her. She turned back to her father and gently laid her hand on top of his. He brought his hand to his face, pinching the bridge of his nose, his eyes squeezed tight. She saw his bottom lip quiver and she did her best to stay strong.

"Eleanor, leaving you when you were six to go overseas was one of the hardest things I have ever had to do, but seeing my little girl all battered is much worse. I wish I could turn back the clock and try to work more at being a father and a husband. If I never left for the military, you wouldn't have been through hell. I am sorry I failed you," he sobbed, his head lying on top of their hands. Eleanor reached across, fighting back the pain as she rubbed his arm.

"Please, it wasn't your fault. You haven't failed me; you're here for me right now. I love you," she reassured, as she continued to comfort him.

He raised his head, his blue eyes piercing at her through the tears. "I love you, Ellie, I never stopped loving you. I promise I will never leave you again. You're stuck with me, sweetheart," he smiled slightly, reaching up and cradling her swollen cheek. She smiled the best she could. She had waited her whole life for this moment.

CHAPTER NINETEEN

"Where are you? I know you are in here, little brat! You can't hide from me forever!" he growled, slowly walking into Eleanor's bedroom, the rank of him and his cigarette lingered in the air and flowed t under the bed to where she had crammed herself to the very back, pushed up against the wall.

She tried to breathe as quietly as she could, muffling her tears with the sleeve of her shirt. She could only see his shoes, walking toward her bed, terrified that he would hear how loud her heart was beating. He stopped right beside it and silence filled the room. Seconds passed by like hours. Suddenly he took a drag of his cigarette, quickly dropping to the floor and looked directly at her as he blew smoke from his cigarette right at her face.

"Found you, brat!" he barked, while she coughed viciously from the second-hand smoke. He caught the end of her shirt and started to pull her out. Eleanor began to scream and cry. She begged for her mother to help her. Even though she knew there wasn't any point; her mother never came to save her.

Once he pulled her out, he shoved her on the floor making her sit in front of him. "Do you know what we do to little girls who lie to their mother?" he asked maliciously, rolling up her sleeve.

She tried to pull her arm away but there was no use. He was stronger than her. She looked away, knowing what was coming next. She cried and prayed to God to take her away. He grabbed her face making her look at him. "Answer me!" he shouted, slapping her across the face. She screamed out in pain, not answering. "Since you can't answer me, I guess I will show you!" he chuckled, taking his cigarette and slowly bringing it to her arm...

"Eleanor, wake up! Wake up honey, please," a muffled voice said as Eleanor frantically woke up, tears rolling down her face, body covered in sweat. She slowly rolled onto her back, causing shooting pains to spread throughout her chest. She let out a whimper, as she looked for the voice who was calling for her.

Andrew appeared next to her hospital bed rubbing her arm as he grabbed her waist gently helping her sit up more. She automatically looked at her arm, where the tiny burns were.

He silently handed her a glass of water. She took it but didn't meet his eyes. "Thank you," she whispered, sighing heavily. She hadn't had one of those dreams in such a long time.

"Are you okay?" he asked, gently sitting on the bed next to her. He took the arm she was holding against her chest. He lightly took his index finger, tracing the burns. She lifted her eyes to watch him trace the marks, her breathing starting to slow. Surprisingly, his touch calmed her instantly.

She just nodded, not sure what to do with herself at the moment. He gently lifted her chin, making her gaze into his eyes. His hair was a mess and his eyes were glazed over, but God, did he still look gorgeous. Her eyes grew soft at his features. She didn't want to think what she had done to him, all the hurt she caused him because of her past.

"Sorry," she replied as she slowly slumped into the pillows. "I had a nightmare..." she just looked back down toward the burns. She hated that they plagued her dreams. She felt that nothing will ever be enough to make the pain go away.

"Do you want to talk about it?" he asked, rubbing her hand, his other hand still on her arm.

Tears well up in her eyes, "Just one of the ..." she mumbled, as she slowly sunk farther down into her bed. She wished that she could just vanish, if would make it so everyone would stop worrying about her. She knew she wasn't worth it.

Andrew didn't say anything but his cheeks and muscle clenched. He started to get up. She grabbed his hand. She looked at him with wide eyes... "Please don't leave!" she pleaded.

"Honey, of course I won't, I haven't," he said, as he pulled his duffle bag from under the bed. He sat down next to her bed, setting the duffle bag next to him. She was awestruck and confused.

"What about Trevor? Who has been watching him?" she asked, concerned.

"Ryan has graciously moved into my place while I stay here with you. Actually, Trevor demanded I stay with you," Andrew confessed, with a small smirk.

"How much longer will I have to stay here?" she asked. She could talk better; her lip had decreased in size dramatically. She hadn't seen her face yet and frankly didn't want to. Her swollen eye was almost healed. She could now open it most of the way.

"A couple more days, the doctor is impressed at how fast you're recovering," he smiled. Andrew paused as he bit his bottom lip as he looked out the window. As he turned back, his eyes got wide. "Eleanor..." he paused. "I love you and I will tell you every day for the rest of my life. You've made me feel things that I didn't think were possible. When I see you, I'm home; you're the air I breathe, and the ground beneath my feet. I've never had my heart flutter the way it does when I see you, kiss you, and hold you. You have opened my heart and mind to a world where there are no doubts. You make me want to be a better man than I can ever be," he smiled, his eyes clouded with emotion.

Eleanor held her hand up, his romantic confession was getting the best of her. The strong pull in her chest, physically hurt. She thought the first time it was a dream, she never expected for him to actually fall in love with her. Now that her mind is clearer, the thought of him loving her scared the crap out of her.

"Andrew I can't..." she cried, turning away from him.

"Why the hell not? Eleanor, look at me," he said, raising his voice. "You can't keep pushing me away when things become deeper between us."

"You don't understand...."

"I understand you more than you know yourself! I know you love me and you're scared if you actually say those words, something will happen and I will leave you, but I am telling you this...I won't," he interrupted her. She looked up at him with fury in her eyes; she hated that he was right, but was she willing to risk losing this man? She knew she wanted to tell him, but why now? She couldn't help but feel his push again. She knew he was only trying to help, but this time it was too much for her to bear.

"Why do you keep pushing me so hard, why now? This isn't fair! You know I need time, for Pete's sake I'm in a hospital bed! I just-," she snapped, then sighed, drained from her emotions. "Thank you Andrew, you don't know how much those words have touched me, but I'm sorry, I can't say them back."

His eyebrows furrowed, but his expression confused. His mouth agape, he turned away biting on the inside of his cheek. The room grew silent, Eleanor's mind going frantic. She had no idea what was going on inside his head. She was afraid at what he would say next.

"Andrew you know how I feel about you," she stopped. "I'm just scared. At least I'm being honest with you."

Andrew's shoulders grew stiff, his jaw clenched as he turned toward the window. He got up from the chair and reached for his jacket. She could see how much he was struggling. He started walking towards the door but stopped right in front of her bed, turning to her. "If you know you love me, I don't understand how you can't just say it...I guess maybe you don't," he said in a flat voice, his pride hurt. Without another glance he walked out the door, leaving the room like an icebox.

Eleanor's eyes widened and she watched him walk out the door. "What the hell just happened?"

Andrew walked into the local diner to meet Ryan, previously relaying yesterday's events to Ryan about him and Eleanor. He did his best not to think about what was said. He wanted to kick himself for how arrogant he acted. He was so stubborn and didn't want to admit she was right about everything. Why was he trying to push her? He knew damn well she loved him. Why wasn't that enough for him?" he thought, racking his brain.

"Hey guys," Andrew said, forcing a smile.

"You're a fool for being here," Ryan said bluntly, as Andrew sat down.

"Well, it's nice to see you too," Andrew rebutted, as he turned to Trevor who looked up from his book; staring him down with intense eyes. "Hey Trev-what's wrong?" Trevor rolled his eyes, letting out a big huff then went back to reading his book. Andrew was shocked about Trevor's attitude. "Okay, what the hell is going on? Why are you both mad at me?"

"First of all, I told Trevor what you told me. Second of all you should have known better. Haven't I taught you anything?" Ryan bickered, Andrew rolling his eyes. You confessed your love to her, but it was the wrong timing man." Ryan argued, taking a drink of his water. Ryan leaned back, putting both hands up in front of him, "Hey, you need to relax...she wasn't ready to say it back, so what? Hell, we all know she loves you, but you know her past, you know those are powerful words to her. Isn't being there for her enough right now?" Ryan hashed out, hitting Andrew like a storm.

"I just wanted to tell her how I felt. I didn't know it was going to result into this," he sighed, leaning over the table putting his head into his hands, running his fingers through his hair.

"Just go back and talk to her before we leave," Ryan retorted, as he flipped over the menu even though he already knew what he was going to get. He got the same thing every time.

"What do you mean before we leave?" Andrew asked, raising his eyebrow, confused.

"Didn't my dad tell you? We got invited by his friend to join their expedition. We will be leaving at the end of the month to go toward Nova Scotia out on the Bay of Fundy for about six months," Ryan stated, not looking enthused.

Andrew's mouth dropped, and he sighed heavily leaning back in his chair. He looked at Trevor. It would be the longest time they would be spent apart. His stomach turned at the thought of being away that long from Trevor and Eleanor. He knew he had to make it right before he left. He had a little over a month before he left to make amends with her. As for Trevor, Andrew knew that Eleanor would watch him, with the help of her father and Amelia. She wouldn't want him to go anywhere else. At least Andrew knew that Eleanor loved Trevor. Now he was having more doubts than ever on her feelings toward him.

CHAPTER TWENTY

Finally after a grueling week, Andrew helped Eleanor hobble up the steps to her cottage. He wanted to carry her, but she was adamant about doing it herself. The sun felt warm on his back and it gave him a sense of closure that the end to all this madness was over. Eleanor was doing remarkably well for her injuries. She still had months of rehab in front of her, but she was on the road to recovery. Andrew's throat constricted knowing that he wouldn't be there for her during that time. He was grateful for her father showing up in her life at this time. Andrew would feel somewhat better about leaving for his long voyage knowing that her father would be there to protect her.

"How about I make you a comfy chair out on the deck? You haven't been outside in a while and I think fresh air would do us both good," Andrew suggested, looking toward the patio door.

Amelia walked in behind them, carrying some bags. "I think that is a perfect idea! I have made some goodies for us today as a welcome home for Elle."

Andrew watched Eleanor gaze at both of them as

tears cascaded down her cheeks. Andrew's heart did a flip as he wiped them with his thumb. "You deserve this sweetheart."

Andrew wanted to say "I love you," but after that day, they avoided the subject like the plague. He was so afraid to bring it back up. The day after the fight, he visited her after getting that lecture from Ryan. When he walked in she was with her father laughing about something private between them. As soon as he heard her laugh, the sound pierced his heart and the anger he once had trickled away. She turned to him, noticing his presence, her face still battered. Her smile dropped but his didn't, he knelt down beside her hospital bed, taking her hands into his. "You're so beautiful," he whispered, pouring his heart out in every word. Her face went from a blank slate to her sexy smirk, cheeks becoming flustered. She slowly and carefully leaned toward him and gave him a gentle kiss. He was shocked because she was kissing him in front of her father and he thought she was still peeved at him. Once their lips met it was like planets colliding even for as brief as it was. She pulled back staring straight into his eyes; he knew then he was a goner. She turned back to her father with her hand on his.

Trevor excitedly burst through the door of the cottage, startling everyone. He peered around the house till he saw Eleanor. He rushed toward her, almost in a tackle. Andrew hopped to his feet to see if she was hurt, but all he could hear was the sweet, joyous laughter between the two.

"Ellie, I am so happy your home!!" Trevor shouted, as he pulled her tighter in the hug. Andrew wanted to tell Trevor to be careful, but seeing Eleanor smile so brightly, her eyes so happy he stopped himself. He saw Ryan walk in slowly behind, shutting the door. He looked drained, though he smiled slightly at Andrew. Andrew knew that something was still off. He mouthed the words, "Are you okay?" Ryan nodded, in agreement, but Andrew knew he was lying.

Trevor, Amelia, and Eleanor headed outside but Andrew stopped Ryan before he could reach the door. Ryan's head dropped. "I don't want to talk."

"Come on, you have been in this weird funk for the last few weeks. What's up? You and..."Andrew was about to ask when Ryan put his hand up to stop Andrew.

"I told you I didn't want to talk," Ryan snapped, rubbing his hands through this hair. He walked over putting both hands down in front of the sink, lowering his head in defeat. Andrew was utterly confused. It wasn't like Ryan to keep quiet. They'd been best friends for so long, there were no secrets. For Ryan to keep this to himself, only meant it really got under his skin. Andrew walked up, leaning his body against the counter next to Ryan. Andrew was patient; he knew Ryan would open up in time. Ryan looked up at Andrew with tormented eyes that aged him ten years.

"Would you like a beer?" Andrew asked, breaking the silence.

"I would love one," Ryan stated with a weak smile. Andrew grabbed two beers, sitting at the kitchen table, waiting for Ryan to join him.

"Okay ...what the hell is wrong with you? I don't like seeing you like this. What happened?" Andrew asked, as he squared himself toward Ryan. For a brief moment Ryan appeared to be weak, small in front of Andrew.

Ryan closed his eyes as he sighed. "You remember crooked tooth Rachel, right? Well did you know that is who owns the floral shop now?" Ryan asked.

Andrew became confused, "Umm... yeah I know. I talk to her quite a bit. She is still nice as she was in high school."

"You were nice to everyone in high school. I didn't know... that was her." Ryan admitted.

"You're the one that gave her that stupid name. How could you have not known it was her?" Andrew asked.

"I don't know. I'm a man and I'm oblivious to these things. It's not like I go to the floral shop like you do. She looks way different now, how was I supposed to know she was the same person!" Ryan ranted, throwing his hands up in the air.

"That's sure a lot of excuses." Andrew laughed. "So... did something happen that day on the beach that I don't know about?" Andrew asked.

Ryan sighed heavily this time, taking a big swig of his beer. He set it down to look out the window, avoiding Andrew's gaze. He took another swig of his beer and then turned back to Andrew. Andrew had never seen his friend turned over like this about a girl. Andrew stilled himself when Ryan open his mouth.

"No."

"What?" said astound. "You're lying."

Ryan looked up at the ceiling, and then looked back at Andrew shaking his head. "No, I'm not. Just been a long week okay. Now...I think it's time we should head outside. I don't think Eleanor wants me to keep you from her." Ryan said with a small smirk as he stood up and left to join the others, Andrew following behind. Andrew was flabbergasted that Ryan lied to his face, but finally decided that when he wanted to talk, he would.

"By the way, this came in the mail for you," Andrew

said breaking into Eleanor's thoughts, as he handed her a white envelope that stated it was from the police station.

She took a deep breath and opened it. Everyone became quiet as she read it. Her hands shook as she was making out what it meant. Eleanor read it twice to make sure she understood all the proceedings. "They're asking me if I want to press charges on the accounts of attempted murder, child abuse, and parental negligence," she gulped loudly, staring down at the paper. "You don't think he would have really killed me do you? Do you think my mother would have allowed him to go that far?" she asked, hoping her answer to herself wasn't right.

She gazed up at Andrew because her question was directed toward him. His face drooped and his mouth turned into a frown. He looked down avoiding her. "I'm sorry, but when I got there, it didn't look like he wasn't planning on stopping," he mumbled, the last of his words. "What are you going to do?"

"I don't know. They're in enough trouble as it is and I know even with my charges they're going to be locked away for a while. I really don't want to go to court and have to relive my past. I have been trying so long to forget it," she cried, staring down at the paper. Rachel nodded in agreement, but when Eleanor noticed Andrew didn't comment, she looked up at him. His hands were clenched into a tight fist as he gazed out the kitchen window. She was hesitant to ask what he thought, even though she could see his answer by his body language. His shoulders and arms were stiff. His eyebrows furrowed together. She knew he wanted her to take them to court and make them pay for everything they did to her.

"I think you should think about it before making your final decision," he said at last, his voice deep and rough, holding in his anger. "Can you do at least one favor for me?" he asked, his tone direct. She could only nod. "Get a restraining order placed on them," He added. "Just as extra precaution for when I am gone for work months at a time."

"Yes, I think that will make us both feel a lot better, but..." she paused. "I wouldn't just get it for me. I would get one for you and Trevor as well," she stated, glancing at Rachel who nodded in agreement again. She was going to do it no matter what. However, the restraining order wasn't her problem right now. She had this uneasy feeling wash over her when Andrew made his last comment. Was there something he wasn't telling her?

Suddenly an angry voice bellowed from outside, shaking Eleanor to the core. Andrew and Amelia rushed to the windows to look, however, Eleanor already knew who it was. She turned to look at Amelia with horrified look on her face.

I will go talk to him," Amelia said grimly.

"I am right here if you need me," Andrew stated, placing his hand on her shoulder. She nodded, grabbed her jacket and headed outside. Andrew helped Eleanor toward the window so she could get a better look. Her uncle's face grew pale at the sight of Amelia walking down the steps.

"So this is where you ran off to... to help that bitch of a cousin who steals from others!" Ron bellowed, as he marched toward her.

Amelia stood her ground. "It's better here than living into a family that is wretched with greed!"

"So everything I have done for you, meant nothing?

You lousy brat!" he snapped, taking a step forward. Amelia held her ground.

"What have you ever given me, beside material crap! That is all that you and Mom ever cared about! Now you're obsessed with this money that doesn't even belong to you. Let it go, otherwise you will end up like your sister!" She snarled back.

Her father's lip curled, shaking profusely. "What did you do to her? I knew she should have ended Eleanor when she got the chance," He barked, rubbing his hand through his balding head.

"End her? She came here to kill her?" Amelia asked, gulping down a huge ball of air. Goosebumps rose throughout her body.

To Amelia's surprise her father laughed. "No, she isn't that dumb! She was going to put her in her place. I guess she already did, didn't she. I noticed she isn't out here, is she?" He chuckled, his belly shaking.

Eleanor watching from the window, made a quick move to the door, but Andrew held her back. "No, he isn't worth it." Eleanor balled up her hands tight into fists, wishing she could pounce on her uncle and smack him.

"She might look rough, but you should see your sister and her boyfriend. Which by the way if you want to, they're down in prison waiting for state trial," She snapped back, a smile forming on her face when her father's face turned white."I don't think they're going to go down for this without ratting you out, don't you think?"

Ron opened and shut his mouth a couple times. His face going from white to red, back to white, "She wouldn't dare, after all I have done for her!" He bellowed as fear crossed his face as he slowly started backing up to his car.

Just then, Jameson's truck pulled beside Ron's B.M.W. Jameson had a fierce gaze on Ron as he stepped out of the vehicle. Ron backed up quickly stumbling on his own feet, flying backward on the ground.

"What the hell are you doing here? I thought you were dead?" Ron asked, his voice trembling.

"Abby never told you? I was never dead," Jameson said sarcastically, smiled as he walked toward Ron. Ron quickly got up on his feet and waddled to his driver side door. At that point, Eleanor and Andrew came outside onto the porch. Andrew walked to Jameson's side, both crossing their arms. Ron took one look at Andrew, remembering him from the first time they met and began to sweat.

"Now...you can leave here peacefully, never showing your face again or I'm calling my buddy at the station to have him pick you up for trespassing...your choice," James bellowed walking a step closer to Ron.

Ron glanced at Amelia to see her face stern and unchanged by the events. He glanced up at Eleanor letting out a giant huff, then turned to Jameson and Andrew and nodded. Without another word, he quickly got in his car and left. When his car was out of sight, Eleanor felt she could finally breathe. Jameson reached Eleanor on the porch and wrapped her in a hug. Eleanor began to laugh, making everyone stop and stare with confusion. She laughed until there were tears streaming down her face. Everything was finally over.

"I am just so relieved," her body and spirit felt so alive. She didn't feel the need to constantly be on alert anymore; she was free.

The rest of the evening was a celebration. Everyone got champagne and toasted. As the sun began to set over the chilly night, everyone gathered around the fire pit, watching the ash dance into the sky. Eleanor looked off into the distance, in a trance of her own thoughts. She felt that the eye of the storm was over but had a dull nagging feeling in her gut that it wasn't done with her yet.

CHAPTER TWENTY-ONE

Eleanor couldn't face the crowd at the moment. Everyone she knew was at Andrew's house for a summer barbeque, with all their close friends and family. Eleanor knew she couldn't get very far with her crutches so she hid out in Andrew's shed. Don't get her wrong, she loved being surrounded by loved ones. Ever since the incident Andrew had been slightly smothering her, and not that she didn't love it, but it was nice to have some quiet time before the festivities really started.

She remembered the memory they had in the shed when they first met. Eleanor glanced around and frowned, remembering that they didn't get any further finding out about Mary and Claire's past and relationship with one another. The smell of fresh wood shavings filled her lungs. It brought her serenity with the distant sound of the waves crashing upon the rocks. She couldn't believe how messy it still was in here. Boxes scattered all around, hardly touched. Suddenly she noticed a parchment paper on the table. As she picked it up, she noticed from Andrew's work. She glanced at it closely, heart sinking deeper and deeper in her chest.

Departure: August 3rd 5 a.m.
Arrival home: January 3rd @ 8 a.m. (Weather permitted.)

It stated Andrew was leaving for roughly six months, sailing off of Nova Scotia. She frantically glanced at the date he would be leaving. Two weeks from today's date. Her blood boiled. Was he not going to tell her about it? Why wouldn't he? Who was going to watch Trevor? Surely he would have told her, she thought. She couldn't help but feel betrayed. As she continued to glance over the paper, something hit the sun rays just right, making it shine into her eyes. She shielded her eyes from the glare as she cautiously hobbled toward it. Slowly bending down, she noticed an oval shaped locket made of sterling silver. There was a rose engraved in the front with exquisite designs around the edges. Eleanor gasped at how gorgeous it was. She lightly rubbed her thumb over it feeling the perfect edges of the design. She knew it had to be old. She flipped it over and on the back was engraved, For Claire. Eleanor couldn't help but open it up and see who was inside. She slowly and ever so gently opened the locket to find a vintage picture of what looked to be Claire and some man, she squinted. She shook her head. "That looks like Ryan!" she gasped. He had the same boyish grin, and emerald eyes. She continued her search.

Andrew searched through the small crowd to find Eleanor. The sun started to set over the horizon leaving a beautiful lasting glow of shades of purple, blue and pink. The breeze was a little chilly swirling smells of salt off the ocean and lilacs that were planted at the sea edge. Andrew knew that Eleanor couldn't have wandered that far with the cast. Suddenly he spotted her underneath the glow of the tea lights that surrounded the old wooden swing.

Andrew slowly walked toward her, sitting next to her on the swing, Eleanor never glanced up. His heart stopped when she handed him the paper. Andrew skimmed over the paper, knowing full well it was his departure paper about the lobster expedition.

She glanced up at him with despair in her eyes, and his heart sank in his chest. He never wanted her to find out this way. He was about to open up his mouth to explain when she put her hand up.

"How long have you known?" she asked, searching into his eyes.

Andrew looked back down at the paper; silence filled the void like dense fog. Andrew was fearful of telling her the truth which she could have sensed because she turned her head away and looked into the approaching darkness.

"Andrew, please," she begged.

"For about a couple weeks, I-," he blurted, but stopped when she turned and put her finger on his lips, staring intently at them. Andrew froze not knowing what she was going to do. He had a thousand thoughts roll through his mind, but they all vanished when she looked into his. Her eyes showed sadness, but also a fire. Eleanor's eyes dropped to his lips and at this time so did her finger. She slowly leaned toward him and Andrew's pulse went wild. Her lips gently touched his and it felt as if his heart had exploded like fireworks in the humid summer night sky. Her lips moved urgently against his, making his growing desire to take her right there even more powerful. Too soon she pulled away, "Thank you."

Andrew grew perplexed. "What?"

Eleanor smirked. "Don't get me wrong, I was pissed when I found this, but the more I thought about it, it made me understand why you didn't tell me..." She paused. "Andrew if you told me that you were leaving a couple weeks ago, it would have destroyed me," she said sternly. She took Andrew's hand in both of hers squeezing it tightly, dropping the paper, letting it swirl onto the ground. "I wish I would have known sooner, but like I said I know why you did it," she added.

Andrew sighed leaning back in the chair. Eleanor kept surprising him and he felt guilty for not giving her more credit.

"Who is going to take Trevor? Don't answer that, because I am. No one else!" she demanded, with the utmost determined look in her eyes. Andrew couldn't help but smile.

"There would be no one else I would rather have watch him. You already have his heart and mine." Andrew smiled taking her hand into his. She looked down at their hands then back up smiling at him. His heart swelled in his chest. "How did I get so lucky?" Andrew smirked, making Eleanor blush.

"I think it's the other way around!" she giggled, slowly leaning back into Andrew for another kiss; once again igniting the fire deep inside. His pants became tight as she nibbled on his lower lip, making him moan.

He pulled away taking a deep breath. He watched

Eleanor in the candle light as her eyes blazed with new sense of desire and lust, that he never seen before. "There is something I would like to try before you leave," she said, in her most sultry voice. He would take her right then and there if there weren't so many people here. Could she really mean what he thought she meant? They never went farther than making out which he was okay with because he knew she needed time, but with her talking so seductive now, he was going to have trouble waiting anymore.

Andrew never wanted to leave this moment. He felt that everything now was falling into place. He promised himself when he made it back from the lobster expedition that he was going to marry Eleanor; he would do everything in his power to return to her no matter what the ocean would throw at him.

CHAPTER TWENTY-TWO

Ryan coughed, breaking Eleanor's trance on the necklace she was holding as she sat at the picnic table, while Andrew and Trevor were making smores. "Everything okay Elle?" Ryan asked, concerned, sitting down next to her. She hadn't told Andrew about the necklace yet. She got side tracked once Andrew's lips touched hers, but she knew she wanted to tell Ryan about it though.

"Ryan, does this man look familiar to you?" she asked, holding up the necklace towards him. He took it from her hand and examined it carefully. She saw his eyes widen. He glanced at her and back at the locket again.

"That is my grandpa, Owen Alistair. Who is the woman? Where did you find this?" Ryan asked, as questions cascaded from his mouth.

She couldn't help but giggle at his outburst. "That woman is my grandma, Claire. Is your grandpa here? Do you think I can talk to him?" she asked, as she continued to gaze at the locket.

Without another word, Ryan grabbed Eleanor's hand and helped her get up and she hobbled after him, off in search of Ryan's grandfather; a key to all their questions.

Eleanor and Ryan found Owen sitting next to Ryan's mother around the fire. Ryan set out a seat for Eleanor next to him. Ryan's mother Olivia and grandfather became quiet, as if they could sense that they were needed. Eleanor handed Owen the locket. He gasped, looking between Eleanor and Ryan. Eleanor couldn't imagine what must have been going through his mind.

"Where did you find this?" he asked, his voice shaky as he intensely gazed upon it.

"How do you know my grandmother and what happened between Mary and Claire?" Eleanor asked, as the flames whirled between them. He reached over to take her free hand, placing his other hand on top of hers.

"My dear, you look just like her when she was your age. She had a fiery rage inside her; if she wanted to do something, she did it, nothing would stop her. I am sorry to hear of her passing, but you know she will be always with you. That sapphire ring around your neck proves that." He sighed. "May I see it, dear? I remember the day I gave that to her," he smiled morosely, gently taking the necklace, dangling it in front of his face. He rubbed his hand down his face. Eleanor was afraid that he would start tearing up but instead he surprised everyone by laughing, not just any laugh, but a deep belly laugh that shook his whole body. Eleanor couldn't help but giggle as well. "Oh, Claire was always stubborn. Everyone and their mother knew that we belonged together, but she couldn't see it. Not that I was broadcasting my love for her myself, but I guess I was just more obvious showing it then she was," he chuckled.

"We first met when she moved here when she was seventeen. Her house was three houses down from mine. Mary's was next to her on the right. Even though Claire was eight years older than Mary, they spent a lot of time together. Claire would often babysit Mary multiple times a week and even when she wasn't they would still find a way to be together," he stated, glancing at Andrew. Trevor gathered by the fire now, sitting between Andrew and Eleanor.

"However, when Claire turned twenty, her father got a job in Wisconsin. By the end of summer she was gone. I remember Mary and me standing by the curb watching their car drive in the distance. It took every ounce of me not to cry in front of Mary. Mary, however, stood there pouting, tears rolling down her face as she clutched my arm. I reassured her that Claire would come back and three years later that is what she did." Owen stated, pausing to catch his breath. His voice was soothing, putting everyone around the fire in a spell. All eyes were on him. The only sound you heard between pauses was the crackle or the fire and the faint crashing of the waves against the rocks.

"When she came back, her beauty radiated over everyone and everything. I fell more in love with her from that moment on and knew with all my power that I was going to marry her. Claire and Mary picked up right where they left off. Five years later she moved back to Hope Harbor, within the first year she moved back, we were engaged. I was more than ready to marry the woman who stole my heart. The day was set, Mary was the maid of honor and Andrew was the ring bearer," he stopped sighing sadly.

"When the time came, the musicians started to play

but my dear, sweet Claire never walked down the aisle. That was the last time I ever saw her. She left me a letter that I didn't see until I got back to the dressing room at the church. It merely stated that her father didn't approve of the wedding and came for her from Wisconsin demanding her to return home. She didn't have a choice I guess. I just wish she would have told me sooner. I would gladly have gone with her, even though I was part of the problem. I swore I left my heart at the altar that day, but God had other plans," he ended with a bittersweet smile.

Eleanor didn't know whether to believe him or call him a liar. She didn't know her grandmother's story and she couldn't believe that he would make up some story like that. Her chest ached for Owen, but she couldn't imagine being left at the altar or left at all by the person she was so devotedly in love with. She got up and sat next to Owen took his hand and gave him a gentle squeeze.

"You never forget your first love. I know she didn't mean to hurt me. Your grandmother was an amazing woman," he smiled as he looked down at her chest, his eyes becoming misty.

Eleanor looked down at her grandmother's engagement ring that dangled from the silver chain. "Is this what you gave her?" Eleanor asked, as she took it off from around her neck, handing it to Owen's weathered hand.

He sobbed lightly. "Yes, I can't believe she carried it all these years," he smiled, tears flowed down his face, his wrinkles shining in the flame of the fire. "She gave this to you?" he asked, his voice becoming raspy. Eleanor nodded. She was afraid if she spoke, she would burst into tears. He brought the necklace to his chest as he looks up into the night sky. "Thank you God! This has brought me so much closure. All things were meant to be. You're meant to bring this to me! You belong here my dear and God knows you belong with him."

CHAPTER TWENTY-THREE

"Someone is an eager beaver this morning." Ryan chuckled as he got out of Andrew's truck. Andrew's eyes followed Ryan's to see Eleanor standing at the dock with a thermos and a box of donuts. Andrew's heart burst in his chest like a fourth of July firework. Ryan's dad, Paul met them at the entrance of the dock with a smug look on his face.

"What is that look?" Andrew asked suspiciously, narrowing his eyes at the older man. Andrew always looked up to Paul as a father figure and he knew that Paul saw Andrew as a son and had no problem pushing Andrew's buttons once in a while.

"I forgot that we get a beautiful damsel this morning and she is feeding us! Boy-you better marry this girl." Paul chuckled as he walked toward Eleanor, closing the distance between them. Andrew could tell that she overheard the conversation by the pink blooming across her cheeks. Andrew himself blushed, but lucky for him, it was covered by his beard. Silence fell across the waters of the shore, except for the annoying noise of Paul and Ryan chomping on their donuts.

Ryan looked up at Andrew and grinned. "What? Cat got your tongue bud?!" Ryan turned over to Eleanor giving her a wink, which darkened the pink even more on her cheeks.

Andrew glared hard at Ryan, and resisted the rising urge to slug him. As if Ryan could sense it, he just shrugged his shoulders and turned back to his father. Eleanor's eyes didn't leave Andrew's the whole time and he felt as he was going to spontaneously combust right on the dock at five o'clock in the morning.

"This isn't the boat is it?" Eleanor said breaking his thoughts. His head followed her eyes to the small twenty-one foot boat.

Andrew chuckled. "No, this boat will take us out to Lucy."

"Are we all going to be able to fit on the boat?" she asked, looking at the size of the boat then glancing up at Andrew, Ryan, and Paul.

"Don't worry, we will be making two trips. Paul and Ryan will go first with some of the extra equipment and then Ryan will come back and get us."

Ryan and Andrew started packing the boat while Paul went over basic security and safety procedures. Andrew chuckled to himself when he saw Eleanor's eyes get big as Paul explained the steps of an unexpected storm approached and what steps they would take. He wanted to save her from the impending doom of what was yet to come with information on lobstering, but time was of the essence and they needed to head out of port soon.

As the boat headed to Lucy, silence took over once more. It felt more peaceful than compact. Andrew watched Eleanor gaze out upon the water, while Ryan and Paul drifted farther way. He reached out taking her hand.

"Thank you letting me come out with you today." Eleanor said, glancing up at Andrew.

"It was actually their idea," he chuckled. "They'll

probably want to hassle me in front of you while we're miles out at sea. You'll giggle at what they say, while they torture and tease me."

She looked up at him, scrunching her lips together. "I highly doubt that. I am just happy that I'm not on crutches anymore. I would take this knee brace over a cast any day. I hated that people had to tend to me... I wasn't used to it. Everyone has just been so thoughtful and caring. I want to do something to make it up to them."

"You know that everyone in Hope Harbor looks out for one another and they all adore you," Andrew paused. He wanted to say "love," but still wasn't sure how she would react to it. "I know Paul and Ryan think very highly of you and I think that is why they give me such a hard time. They don't want anything to happen to you, even the times we get into fights. More than half the time they took your side instead of mine and that is saying a lot. You have something special about you Eleanor and everyone can see that. I can feel it right now as I'm touching your hand. It's like electricity that you can feel in the air before a storm hits," he said squeezing her hand harder. Andrew took his finger to her chin, pulling it closer to his lips. When she was an inch away, he whispered. "I know you can feel it too...and Eleanor-I want to feel this till the end of time," Andrew didn't give her time to react before gently kissing her lips, lingering his mouth lightly on hers.

"You're not really going to let her drive the boat, are you?" Ryan asked a concerned look on his face. Andrew just laughed as he started baiting the traps with scraps of herring.

"Ryan, if you can drive the boat, she sure as hell will be able to...and will probably be better!" Paul chuckled, his belly jiggling.

Andrew watched Eleanor as she giggled between the two bickering men. Once Paul turned away, Eleanor called out to Ryan. As he turned, she stuck out her tongue like a five-year-old little girl. Ryan gasped as he turned to Andrew. "Are you going to let your woman treat me like that?!"

Andrew laughed harder. "Stop being such a baby. Did you forget your balls are back on shore?" Ryan grimaced, as he slugged Andrew in the arm, only making Andrew laugh harder. "Ryan you need to relax and have some fun, we're only teasing," Andrew added.

Ryan just huffed and got to work, clearing the area for when he would start hauling the traps in. Everyone got into a rhythm as the ocean waves sang against the sky. They crashed into the boat as it went farther out into sea. Andrew could hear the hum over Paul and Eleanor talking about the boat. He couldn't see her face, but could see she was having the time of her life.

"Now take the helm and remember what I told you. I will be right here guiding you through the buoys. There aren't too many out here today so it shouldn't be that difficult. Once you get the hang of it, it will come like second nature to you and Eleanor... I just want to say you're welcome on the boat anytime. You have brought back the light in Andrew's eyes and we're all grateful and blessed that he has you in his life," he said smiling. He shook his head in disgust. "We never really liked Becca. Too high maintenance if you ask me; couldn't really say anything to Andrew about it though. His glare can sear your skin a mile away," he grimaced, wiping his forehead. Eleanor saw Andrew's famous glare once or twice, luckily never directed at her.

Eleanor took the wheel, her hands at ten and two,

thinking that was the way you're supposed to hold it. Her grip was tight, her arms tense. She was in charge of the vessel. Most people wouldn't have thought it was an important feat, but to her it moved mountains. She had never taken charge of her life until Claire died and at this moment she thought it was finally coming together. She finally reached the end of the tunnel, the light before her was an incredible array of blues.

"Captain...permission to enter quarters?" Andrew asked, leaning against the wall of the door frame, after Paul headed out to help Ryan for a while. Andrew had a smug grin across his face which turned Eleanor's face bright red.

"You like what you see, greenhorn?" Eleanor stated sternly, but failed as she tried to hide her giggle.

Andrew's eyebrow's rose as he let out a cough and a chuckle. "Hmm...greenhorn you say. I guess I will have to show just how experienced I am," Andrew whispered seductively in her ear, all the humor gone from his voice, replaced with the most alluring deep tones that could practically take Eleanor's clothes off right there. The cabin started to heat up. She could imagine the taste of his mouth on hers and wanted nothing more to just feel his lips on hers. Beads of sweat formed on her back and between her breasts. Andrew raised his hand while holding his gaze on her as he tucked her hair back behind her ear, then trailed his hand down her neck, lightly grazing it with his fingertips. He didn't stop there, he continued from her neck down her back. It was taking all her power not to combust right there. He lit a fire deep within her belly that she had never felt before which scared and excited her at the same time. He reached the small curve of her back; he hesitated ever so slightly before touching her bottom curves then trailing his hand down her thigh and resting it on the inner part of her knee.

She finally let out her breath in one big huff, making Andrew's gaze drop to her lips. She couldn't help but notice him biting his lower lip. Eleanor's body felt her every pore was producing steam. "That..." Andrew said in an unsteady voice, his breathing ragged. "Was just the tip of the iceberg," Without another word, he faintly brushed his lips against hers, sending a magnitude of ecstasy through her veins shattering her core into tiny pebbles. He pulled away with stars illuminating his eyes and a smirk a mile long. She opened her mouth to say something, but a small moan broke free instead. His eyes turned black, filled with hazy lustful smoke. "There will be more where that came from." He turned to leave as she just sat there, her heart racing in her chest and her head swimming off into the waves. For her heart knew now there was no doubt in her mind any longer. Eleanor's heart won and she knew at that moment she would do everything she could to keep it that way.

The sun slowly began to hover over the horizon as they pulled into the dock. Eleanor thought it was a good thing; there was a hard chill in the air. She couldn't think of anything she wanted to do more than curl up in a blanket with Andrew while sharing a glass of wine.

Shaking away the promising thoughts, she decided that since she spent the day on the boat with the men that she could handle lugging in some lobster traps off the boat onto the dock as well. All the men took their turns hauling equipment off the boat in a silent rhythm. Eleanor struggled as she picked up a lobster trap, aware that she still hobbled with her knee brace. Realizing they were heavier then she expected, she tried her best to act as if she wasn't struggling, dragging her feet across the wooden dock. Her foot hit an unlevel board, making her stumble. She did her best to correct her footing, but it was too late and she screamed as she fell off the dock into the icy water below. Piercing cold surrounded her, sending extremely painful shocks rippling through her body. She reached the surface frantically, looking around at her surroundings. She suddenly felt something touch her side.

"Something touched me!" she screamed, only to hear a chuckle come from behind her.

"Not funny!" she replied, staring at Andrew who was treading water next to her.

"Just a little..." he paused, his expression turning to worry. "Are you okay?" he asked, pulling her into him, which might have been a bad thing for the both of them.

"Oh yeah...I just felt like taking a swim," she said sarcastically as her teeth chattered.

"Let's get out of the water," Andrew said sternly, as he nonchalantly grabbing Eleanor's waist as they both headed for the boat landing.

Eleanor could swim just fine, but she wasn't going to admit it right now, not with having Andrew so close to her. His body radiated heat and the Maine water didn't seem that cold anymore. She felt all the contours of his body, which sent her mind into a fury fantasizing about other places she could feel. She knew she must get away from him soon or otherwise she was going to go ballistic and might do something crazy right then and there.

They hit the boat landing and she started to hobble away as fast as her brace would allow. She met Ryan on the top that was equipped with blankets. She flew into his arms, once she hit the frigid air that sent another rippling effect through her and every part of her body screamed in agony.

"Thank you!" Eleanor exclaimed, through her chattering teeth.

"We knew you must have been a mermaid, but you didn't need to prove it us," Ryan chuckled back. Eleanor squinted her eyes and slapped his arm which only made Ryan laugh harder.

She started briskly walking to her car, knowing she would thank Paul later for the trip, but right now all she was worried about was getting home and into a bath. The thought however stopped her in her tracks. Eleanor's original plan wasn't to go home right away, but while she was on the boat, she got a text from Amelia stating that her mother turned up out of the blue and wanted to talk to her. There was no way Eleanor wanted to go home to that storm. She turned around to see where Andrew was when she was whacked in the face with his chest. Eleanor got a whiff of his cologne and the ocean, her mouth instantly watering. She took a few steps back.

"Is there something wrong?" Andrew asked, with a concerned look on his face, but heat in his eyes.

Eleanor bit her lip. "I can't go home. Amelia has company," she said looking defeated.

"You can come to my house; I have some clothes you can wear," Andrew said instantly, as if that was what he planned on saying all along.

"Okay..." This time she paused. "On one condition."

"Um...okay." Andrew said confused. "What?"

"I make supper."

CHAPTER TWENTY-FOUR

Andrew was happy that Eleanor was sitting in his truck with a blanket on because he was convinced he would crash his truck or run someone over if she wasn't. He couldn't get the image of her soaked body out of his mind. Her curves were beautiful and he could only imagine her skin would be smooth like caramel. Eleanor and he had touched before and cuddled but nothing more intimate. He coughed trying to snap out of his thoughts before she could tell what he was thinking. He turned on the radio to help keep his mind distracted.

"So which one of Amelia's family member is at your house?" Andrew asked.

Eleanor, who was looking out the window at the time, turned to him with a flushed face, making him curious as to what she might be thinking.

"Her mother...she isn't my biggest fan right now. Well, she never was to begin with..." Eleanor said shrugging her shoulders. "I just feel bad Amelia is there to face her alone, but that is what she wanted."

"She wants you to have a break from all of this."

"I know...and what do I do on my break... fall in the water," she laughed, making Andrew's chuckle along. It was one of the sweetest sounds he had grown to love.

"Well...you are, a little clumsy," Andrew teased.

Eleanor gasped as she slapped him playfully on the arm. "I blame you," She chuckled, but became flushed in the face.

"And why is that?" Andrew asked piqued as to what her answer might be.

"Because..." she paused, huffing, as if she was trying to find the right words or words at all. "You make me loopy...I can't think or do anything straight when you're around. You've invaded my mind making it into mush which leaves my body out of control. All of this," she waved her hands around his whole body. "Makes me think I'm in a candy store and its Christmas morning. I become all giggly and ridiculous. And the worst thing of all...I like it. I love it, I love being around you. You make me forget and make me want more. You make me feel like I'm the only woman in your eyes," she sighed, a small smile spreading across her face and sincere in her eyes.

Andrew was sure his heart was going to explode right then. "That's because you are, no one holds a candle to you," he said proudly. He watched her take in his words.

She snaked her hand out of her blanket, reached over and took his hand. Andrew smiled brightly at her as he squeezed her hand, and then brought it up to his mouth, giving it a light kiss.

By the time they reached Andrew's house the sun finally set, only leaving the soft glow of the solar lights up his pathway. They made a mad dash to the front door where he quickly pulled both of them in. Eleanor was still a little shaky from the water, but Andrew felt like he had a fever. As they walked through his house, he turned on each light in every room. They silently made their way upstairs, Andrew doing his best to push away any thoughts or ideas he had about taking her right then and there on the stairs.

Andrew opened up the dresser drawers and let Eleanor survey them. "Umm...whose are these?" she asked, as she pulled out a skimpy top.

"They're...umm, Becca's," he said cringing. He turned to look at her, as her facial expression turned to hesitant and wary.

"Otherwise...if you don't mind, I have some t-shirts and pajamas you can wear," he stated, hoping to dig himself out of the dog house.

"Yea...why don't you just do that to be on the safe side?" she added, as she continued to dig through the items.

"You can use the shower up here and I will grab you some extra clothes then I will head downstairs and use the guest shower. There are extras of everything, if you need anything. I will put our clothes in the wash when were done," he added, slowly walking out of the room after she gave him a quick nod.

He frantically went into his room pulling clothes out of his closet. He wanted to kick himself for how stupid he was back there. "Becca's clothes, why would I just assume she would be okay with it? I really should get rid of them," he thought to himself. He grabbed a pair of flannel pajamas and a nice thick long sleeve for Eleanor and left it in the bathroom. He still saw the light on in the guest room, which only made him want to kick himself in the butt again. He guessed he would find out if she was pissed at him when she came back down for supper, which she had promised to make.

After her shower, wrapped in a towel, she still seemed to have a hard time relaxing and unwinding knowing she was in Andrew's shower and he was just down stairs. Her fantasies ran wild. With a sigh she glanced at the clothing that was laid out for her. One is Becca's and the other is Andrew's. She couldn't deny that Becca had a great sense on style, but the size on the other hand was an issue.

"Did this girl eat at all?" she muttered, to herself as she held up the most decent shirt she could find. She struggled as she tried putting it on but it was no use. God granted her a bigger bosom then Becca's and there was no way the shirt was going to fit over her chest. She let out a sigh. The only two items left were underwear and yoga pants. She knew they'd been washed but she didn't feel comfortable wearing some other woman's thong. With a defeated huff, she pushed Becca's clothes aside and put on the nice warm long sleeve, which was more like a night gown than a shirt. She didn't want to go commando, but it was her only reasonable choice. A light automatically came on and she chuckled at the thought of what she was about to do. She pulled down the shirt a little more and made a quick dash to Andrew's room, where he would be in for a treat later.

Minutes later, she came down the stairs to hear

sound of pots and pans rattling. She briskly walked into the kitchen to see Andrew in his own rhythm while cutting onions.

"I thought I was making supper tonight?" she asked, with a mischievous grin on her face. Andrew peered up and forced the knife a little harder than he meant into the cutting board. His cheeks became flushed and he gave a shy smile, which sent Eleanor right to the moon.

"I see you didn't go with Becca's clothing," he stated, continuing to smile as he set the knife down and walked around from behind the island.

"No, they didn't fit in some areas," Eleanor said blushing. The eyes on that man and the way he was looking at her could kill.

"That's okay...I like this way better!" he smiled brighter, as he pulled her into a hug, his hand roaming all over her back and bottom. He pulled her head upward as he laid his lips on her with a roaring fire shooting through her veins. He was forceful and rough but not too much, and it sent Eleanor's body into a surge of lust. "If you keep kissing me like this, then we will never get to supper," he smiled, as he pulled his face inches from her.

Before Eleanor could think, she muttered. "Supper can wait."

As soon she uttered those words, he lifted her up, and she wrapped her legs around his waist. Her lips were back on his once more and for the first time, neither one of them were slowing down. Eleanor never craved something or someone more in her life then she did with Andrew right then. Her hands swept over his hair, pulling his head deeper into the kiss. Their tongues explored each other and Eleanor craved the intoxicating taste of him. Her grip on his bottom grew and he squeezed her butt in return pulling her tighter into him. Her heart was pounding in her chest and she thought she would rupture before they even started.

They made it into the bedroom somehow; Eleanor didn't even notice they climbed the stairs. Every place that Andrew touched, felt as if she was being scorched by fire. Andrew set her down and started tearing at the button down shirt. He growled, getting fed up with the buttons. In one swift motion, he ripped her shirt, throwing it on the floor as he let out a moan as he gazed upon Eleanor's bosoms in the candle light. He stood there for what seemed like an eternity. Eleanor's breathed erratically and she could feel Andrew's heated gaze consume her body.

"Are you sure about this?" Andrew huffed, staring at her fervently while he tried to catch his breath.

Instead of answering him, she slowly closed the space between them, reached the bottom hem of his shirt and raised it over his torso. Andrew remained silent, letting Eleanor take control. It gave her a new level of confidence, made her feel like a goddess. She swept her hands over his chest and down his torso ever so slowly. Her hands fumbled with his belt buckle. She noticed his hands forming in fists at his sides. She couldn't imagine what she was doing to him and even more she loved it.

Once the belt came off, she slowly unzipped his pants and pulled them down along with his boxers. His erection stood tall and proud, making Eleanor involuntarily lick her lips as a low gasp escaped from her mouth. That sent Andrew over the edge for the moment; he picked her up and set her on the bed, climbing on top of her. She felt of the weight of him and the hardness of his erection against her thigh and again she'd was afraid to burst right there. Andrew began kissing Eleanor's neck sending wave after crashing wave of euphoria through her body, pooling into her lower abdomen. She couldn't help but let out a moan that caused Andrew to become more urgent and rougher with his kisses. He trailed down her neck, across her collar bones and hovered above her right breast. He looked up into her eyes; she could feel the hot breath on her nipple. She grew more impatient and pleaded with her eyes. Andrew's gaze became dark with lust and he groaned as he lowered his lips onto her breast, kissing it. Eleanor let out a loud moan, her body moving under his and a pulse of ecstasy raced through every fiber of her body.

"Please...Please," she whimpered, as Andrew switched from her right breast to her left sending another shock wave through her system. She could feel his hand trace down her stomach and reach for her underwear which was actually his boxers. Once he felt what it was he let out a chuckle.

"I swear, you will be the death of me," he muttered, over her breast as he pulled off the boxers she was wearing. She was now totally naked in front of him. All of the doubts and insecurities she thought she had were gone in this moment. Andrew raised himself off of her so he could see her full figure. As he raised his head back up to her face he uttered,

"You're so beautiful Eleanor and you're mine," he growled, as he lowered himself back onto her and she felt him enter her slowly. She grabbed onto his shoulders feeling the fullness of him inside her. She let out a cry of pure bliss. As Andrew started slowly thrusting into her, her mind and body went crazy. Her hands were all over his back pushing him closer to her so she could feel more of him.

Soon she started feeling this pressure rise as if she was riding a rollercoaster up to the top before they dropped. Her heart and breath became faster and she wasn't sure what was going to happen until the pressure sky rocketed and she climaxed into tiny pieces. Andrew climaxed after, sending both of their bodies into a rhythm of pure ecstasy.

Andrew lay limp on Eleanor's sweaty body as they tried to calm their breathing. He looked up as his head gently rested on her chest, giving her a million dollar smile of satisfaction. Eleanor let out a soft chuckle as she ran her fingers through her hair.

"This is what I have been missing out on? Damn!" she smiled, again as Andrew toyed with her hair.

Andrew gave her a mischievous grin as he dropped her hair and his finger tip traced down her neck to her breast giving it a light squeeze, automatically triggering the pooling in her abdomen again.

"I guess we will have to make up for lost times then," he said his voice thick and husky. "I want you over and over again...for the rest of time," he uttered sternly, looking her straight in the eyes.

She panted, her body ready to go. "I guess we can wait to eat tomorrow."

CHAPTER TWENTY-FIVE

She awoke to the sun shining through the window, cascading an array of color throughout the bedroom illuminating the pictures that hung on the walls. A bright smile crossed her face as she remembered last night and the lack of sleep that she got. It must have been the hot body that laid beside her now, sprawled naked across the bed. She sighed as she gazed at Andrews back, the contours of his muscles and the curvature of his glorious bottom. His breathing was steady and deep. She knew he would be out for a while.

She slowly got out of bed and wrapped herself up in a robe that she found hanging over the chair. She quietly hobbled downstairs to the kitchen where everything was left out from yesterday. She shook her head thinking that it was a dream but she knew for once it wasn't. She began to pick up the food that had been sitting out and tossed it away. Once she gotten everything picked up she took out the essentials to make breakfast and began cooking away. She flipped on the radio and began to sway to the sweet melody of jazz. Her hips swayed along with the saxophone and she was lost in her own little world. The best thing was, she was undeniably happy. Last night was the second biggest step in her life and she didn't regret it. She had never thought she would be able to ever defeat that beast that raged in her mind for all those years. The only thing that she had yet to defeat was saying those three words.

She knew she loved Andrew. Why was it so hard for her to say? Could it be that it made it final or official? If she told him that she loved him there would be no going back. If something happened to him and she was left alone, she wouldn't know how to go on. This was a different kind of love that she never felt before and it still scared her to death. She had never loved a man before Andrew and there was something to be said about your first love. This love never leaves you; that person, that feeling would stick with you for the rest of your life whether or not you stay with them or not.

A low, rough cough broke her thoughts bringing her to the present, to her dancing in the kitchen while their breakfast started to burn. Smoke filled the kitchen, and she blushed as she frantically turned off the burners and flew open the windows bringing in the crisp chill of the morning. Andrew moved next to her working silently trying to save what he could of the eggs and bacon. She couldn't help but glance at the slight smirk that crossed his face.

"What is so funny, Monroe?" Eleanor asked, suspicious and slightly irritated.

Andrew looked up with an innocent face only making Eleanor want to snicker but she tried to keep a straight face. "Oh nothing...just wondering what a certain person was thinking about to burn these innocent eggs."

"Well...it definitely wasn't you. I don't want your ego to get any bigger than it already is," she snapped, back playfully.

"It's been there since the first moment I met you and I don't think it will be going anywhere. It just bought a condo," Andrew stated matter of fact, making Eleanor erupted into giggles as she flung herself into him for an embraced.

She pulled back staring at him, it was on the tip of her tongue. She shouted at herself, "Say it...just say it!"

"I...I..." she struggled, looking at his now hopeful face, but sighed defeated, "I think we should go out for breakfast."

To Eleanor's surprise, Andrew's expression didn't change when she didn't say it, but only remained hopeful which gave Eleanor more hope and confidence in herself.

"Owen insisted on coming over to show you this album. He isn't supposed to be out of the house, but he can be very persistent," Ryan confessed, when Eleanor opened her door, letting Ryan, Owen, and David into her house.

"I still don't know why I had to come Gramps. I have stuff to do at the station." David whined, flopping onto the couch, looking disgusted.

"You will soon find out," Owen said with a nod, tapping his finger against his nose. That just made David grunt, slouching deeper into the couch.

They made their way to the kitchen, pulling out a chair for Owen. Ryan and Eleanor helping him ease into the wooden chair. Once he was settled, Eleanor put the kettle on and tried her best to keep her nervousness to herself.

"I hope you don't mind I have a friend coming over," Eleanor mentioned, as she got the teacups ready.

"Rachel? Why yes...we would be delighted to see her again, right Ryan?" Owen stated, taking the cup from Eleanor as he glanced at Ryan whose face became confused as he blushed.

"Why would I care if she was here or not?" Ryan stated, with a sarcastic tone as he glared at his grandfather.

Owen smirked, "The same reason I brought David here," he said as the sound of the front door opened and Rachel and Amelia walked through both giggling. The couch in the living room made a huge creaking noise as if David frantically got up from the couch. The giggling stopped, Eleanor heard David greet both ladies, followed by silence; both girls and David appeared in the kitchen. Amelia and David both looked flushed and it seemed that Ryan and Rachel were both ignoring each other.

"So Owen you wanted to show me an album?" Eleanor asked, breaking the tension that was strong enough to cut steel.

Owen clasped his hands as he bent down, bringing an old red album out of a grocery bag. His hands shaking as he put it down in front of Eleanor.

"Ryan was helping me look through my old things in the attic and we came across this album that I had when Claire and I were together." Everyone gathered around the table.

Amelia and Rachel pulled up a chair next to Eleanor as she slowly opened the cover. Her heart was pounding in her chest. She had never seen pictures of her grandmother when she was growing up.

"This is Claire and Mary after the first week of Claire moving here." Owen smiled as he caressed the pictures. She couldn't deny that she had a lot of her features; the fierceness of her hazel eyes, or her heart shaped lips.

They took each picture out and passed it to each person around the table. For the next couple hours they shared giggles and belly laughs. Owen even snuck in some baby pictures of Ryan and Andrew.

"You remembered." Eleanor giggled, as Andrew just walked in.

"Remembered what?" he asked cautiously.

Everyone looked up at him except for Ryan, who just passed him the picture of them in diapers playing. "You're lucky you're surrounded by beautiful ladies old man, otherwise I might have to take you outside," Andrew said bending down and giving Owen a big hug.

"You better get all the looks while you still can...those will be the only ones you will see!" Andrew said, trying to collect them. Trevor walked in at that time with something in his hands, shielding it from everyone.

"Awe! What do you have there, buddy?" Eleanor said, reaching Trevor, who was cradling a tiny kitten that was meowing fiercely.

"I think this little one is hungry. Come, bring it over here." Eleanor said gently, unfolding a towel as Trevor placed the kitten inside of it.

Trevor looked at Andrew with his sad puppy dog look. "Can we keep it?"

Andrew bent down to Trevor's level. "Are you ready for the responsibility buddy? Babies are a lot of work."

Trevor nodded his head eagerly. "Yes I promise." Andrew looked up at Eleanor, who couldn't help but smile as she cradled the kitten who was now purring, while she began to warm up some milk.

"Then you can keep it!" Andrew said, embracing Trevor in a hug. Eleanor saw his gaze upon her as she jumped up and down.

Andrew laughed. "I don't know who is more excited, Trevor or Eleanor."

"I think this was a set up!" Ryan stated, gesturing between the Trevor and Eleanor.

"Well I guess no one will never ever know!" Eleanor said, trying to laugh evilly, giving Trevor a high-five.

Ryan looks at Andrew. "See? I knew it!" Eleanor watched Andrew while he chuckled sitting down next to Ryan. Amelia and Rachel continued to look at pictures and listen to Owen talk. Everyone soon was sitting around the table into the late hours of the night as Owen continued to recount memories of his and Claire's younger years.

The sun hadn't rose over the water yet on Hope Harbor as Andrew gazed upon the stillness of the waves. Birds surrounded his senses in beautiful songs, the chill of the wind as it ran through his hair reminded him of Eleanor's fingers. In only a few hours, he would embark on an amazing journey, yet he couldn't help but feel an ache in his chest knowing what he was leaving behind. He knew this day would come and counted down the days, but in some way he felt his heart cracking each day it did. It's not like he hadn't been on these expeditions before. He went on two to three each year, but now since he met Eleanor, that's the only place he would like to be and stay; his home with her.

He closed his eyes as he listened to the gentle rhythm of the waves hitting the dock. He took a deep breath in, trying to calm and steady his nerves. He heard light footsteps approach him on the dock, which brought a smile across his face.

"I thought you would like some coffee," Eleanor stated, handing him a piping hot cup, steam swirling up into the air like a smoke signal.

"I didn't think you would be up yet," he said, taking a sip of coffee.

"I felt you get up," she paused, taking a sip of her own coffee. "Honestly I don't think I got more than three hours of sleep," she admitted. "It's a big day..."

Andrew didn't know what to say, so instead he put his coffee in his other hand and wrapped his arm around Eleanor's shoulder bringing her closed to him. He bent down kissing her head, smelling the sweet aroma of her shampoo, locking it into memory.

"I want you to have something," she uttered, bringing a frame from behind her back, cradling it into her hands so Andrew could see.

It was a picture of the three of them, Andrew, Eleanor, and Trevor. He remembered the memory well. They had a bonfire in the back yard and they were all smiling as they held up smores. "I love this, thank you!" Andrew smiled brightly, taking the picture from her to get a closer view. "I will put this up in the quarters to make all the other men jealous," he chuckled as Eleanor smacked his arm.

"You're horrible!" she laughed.

"Ha- I wouldn't have it any other way." Andrew laughed. Andrew deep down knew he wouldn't either. Even, if he had to do it all over again, all the pain, tears, and hurt. He would go to hell and back to make sure he would stay with Eleanor for always.

"Do we have to leave soon?" Eleanor asked, as her gaze fell upon the waves, taking his hand. Andrew rubbed his thumb over her smooth soft knuckles.

"Yeah..." he answered roughly. He turned to Eleanor getting her attention. "I want to ask you something." Eleanor's eyes went big, thinking he was going to propose to her. He set down the frame and put both of her hands into his. "If anything...anything happens to me, please tell me you will take care of Trevor," he pleaded. He held up his hand, to stop Eleanor as she opened her mouth. "Please. I want you to adopt him and make him part of your family." He pleaded. "I couldn't picture anyone else raising him and he loved you from the first moment...as I did.

Her mouth closed and her eyebrows furrowed and she sighed. "Of course I will. I promise...I just wish you didn't think like that. I'm a nervous wreck as it is..." she whimpered, tears brimming under her lashes.

"I know..." he sighed, pulling her into a deep hug. "I just want to be prepared for anything, but I want you to know," he stated pulling her back, taking her face into his hands. "If anything were to happen, I want you to know I would fight like hell to get back to the both of you because...I love you. I love you so much, and I know you can't say it or afraid to say it but, I don't want to leave without saying it to you. I know you do Eleanor, without a doubt. It's seeping into my pores right as we speak, it pulsates with the crashing of the ocean waves and I feel the same way. I will for now and always love you," he vowed, to her as he crushed his lips into her without giving her a moment to speak. He rubbed his hands through her hair as he felt tears flow down her cheek into his beard. That was enough for him to confirm her feelings. He wouldn't pressure her again when he got back he made a silent prayer and vow as he did for the last month; he would make her his for now and forever...no matter what.

The ground felt heavier with every step she took as

they all headed toward the dock. The sound of her feet hitting the pavement echoed in her head and she didn't know whether she was counting the steps or breaths. She kept her head down as they inched closer and closer. She was doing her damnest to not break down right then and there. She knew Andrew was in good hands and has done this for how long now, but it didn't stop her from feeling every nerve in her body on fire. Once they reached the dock, she didn't expect to see such a big ship, but yet again she forgot how big the expedition was.

There was chaos everywhere; everyone was busy with a job. There was a hum of noise from workers going in and out of the boat and all the families scattered along the dock immersed in their own lives. Ryan appeared with his father, walking up to us with a giant duffle bag over his shoulder.

"Are you ready for this?!" Ryan smiled enthusiastically, slapping Andrew's arm. Ryan's eyes twinkled with vigor, his smile consuming his whole face. The air around him seemed wild like a hurricane and it made Eleanor clutch her jacket a little tighter around herself.

Andrew chuckled as he set his own duffle bag on the damp concrete, and then raked his hand through this hair. He glanced down at Eleanor with somber eyes, then back at Ryan with a half- hearted smile. "Yes and no." he admitted as he chuckled again.

Eleanor suddenly felt someone's hands in hers, giving hers a light squeeze. She turned to see Trevor stand close to her, giving her a gentle smile. It helped subdue her nerves and she felt her shoulders drop; starting to relax. She leaned into a little more, as she laid her head on his shoulder.

Eleanor watched as the men headed onto the boat

to check in and take care of a few things. She admitted she probably wouldn't leave the harbor until she wasn't able to see the boat in sight.

The next hour seemed like a blur, everything was in its place and the crew was set to sail. Men flocked to their families, saying their heartfelt goodbyes. She saw Ryan and his dad off to the side hugging his mom and grandpa. Andrew and Trevor were having a moment off to the side and Eleanor moved away to give them a little privacy. She couldn't help but watch them interact with each other. Neither of them seemed on the verge of tears which she would have expected but when they hugged each other she almost felt the blast of their love fly by her. She couldn't help but smile brightly, tears threatening to flow once more. Andrew put both hands on each side of Trevor's head and kissed his forehead fiercely. He gave him one last hug and then Andrew's eyes caught hers.

As he turned to walk to her, she felt time slow down. Everything around them went silent and she felt they were the only ones there. Once he reached her he gathered her into a big embrace, picking her up and pinning her to him tightly. As he slowly set her down, her hands found the sides of his face. She caressed his cheeks, staring deep into his eyes.

"Be safe." She whispered, as her emotion started to break. She wanted to say those three words that were planted on the tip of her tongue. "Come back to me." She said instead, knowing that he would know what she meant.

He smirked as if he read her mind. "I love you too. I will, I promise on my heart, on the depth of the sea...I will return." With that he sealed his promise with a kiss. She pulled him closer in the kiss, remembering how soft his lips felt on her and the sweet scent of him.

The ship headed out into the vast ocean, cruising on top of the waves looking unstoppable. She took Trevor's hand in hers, bringing it to her heart. The sky grew brighter as it rose from the horizon and she felt part of her heart floated on that ship, feeling it rock with the waves. She breathed in deep, filling her lungs with the salty air. She said a silent prayer, sending it on the wings of a seagull overhead that soared toward the ship that carried the most important thing to her... him.

CHAPTER TWENTY-SIX

(4 months later)

Eleanor clutched the pillow as she sat on her pale blue love seat in the living room as the news played on her TV. She was anxiously waiting for the weather to appear in the broadcast. Hurricane Kelly was wreaking havoc near Cuba and was projected to head up the Atlantic coast. It wasn't supposed to head toward Maine, weakening once it hit around North Carolina. Unfortunately, Eleanor knew weather could be unpredictable at times.

She sighed, sitting back into the couch, trying to sink into it. The last months really were a trial for Eleanor. Not just because Andrew was gone but she was also in charge of Trevor. They had an amazing relationship, but she could tell Andrew's absence was wearing thin on them both. They even had their first fight last week which left Eleanor in tears and Trevor storming off to the neighbor's house. It wasn't even a real fight she felt as she thought back on it. A miscommunication between them turned into an all-out battle. She knew that no one could take back the words that were said, but she believed if anything, the fight brought them closer together.

"Hurricane Kelly has left Cuba and now is on the path toward Florida's coast. It hasn't weakened but hasn't accelerated either. We will have further weather updates when we come back from a commercial," the female meteorologist stated, as she stood in front of the projection. Eleanor grunted with impatience as she flipped through the channels to find a different news station that would have the weather on. She was interrupted with a knock at the door, and she didn't have time to get up before Rachel walked in.

"Hey sweetie!" She greeted, her as she turned to see what she was watching. "Girl, you need to stop obsessing over the hurricane. It's not going to hit us!" she exclaimed, grabbing the remote from Eleanor's hands as she turned off the TV and walked into the kitchen. Eleanor huffed, but she knew Rachel was right, so she got up and headed to the kitchen where Rachel already was pouring two glasses of wine. Rachel sat down the two glasses then sat down herself as she took a big long sip. Eleanor raised her eyebrow,

"Did you have a bad day?" she asked, as she sat across from her.

Rachel looked at her confused, "Umm...no. I just really love wine." She smirked. Eleanor sensed that Rachel had been on edge since Ryan and Andrew left. She still didn't know what happened between her and Ryan that night. She brought it up once and that didn't go very well so she didn't want to pry anymore. However now, Eleanor had a feeling that Rachel might have feelings for him. It turned out, Benjamin and she broke up a little while after the event at the beach and Eleanor couldn't help but wonder once again if it was because of Ryan.

"Are you okay sweetie...you seem not yourself lately?" Eleanor asked concerned. Rachel took another big swig of wine before nodding her head yes. Eleanor wasn't convinced.

"How about you spend the night?" Eleanor asked Rachel as she poured her second glass of wine.

She shrugged her shoulders. "Why not!? I have another pair of clothes in the car with me, and another bottle of wine!" She grinned and wiggled her eyebrows. Eleanor couldn't help but burst out laughing.

"I am so sorry, but I am taken!" Eleanor laughed.

"I can change that!" Rachel yelled, running after Eleanor. Eleanor clomped into the living room, grabbing a pillow to throw at her. "Girl, don't spill my wine!" she laughed as she flopped onto the couch. "We definitely needed this." Rachel added, running her hand through her hair.

"I agree! With Trevor at his friend's house tonight, it's nice not to be alone. So what is up girl? Are you seeing someone new and not telling me?" Eleanor asked as she took a big gulp of wine, coughing as she slightly choked on it. Rachel looked at Eleanor like she was crazy.

"No, not since Benjamin, I need a break from men for a while." She admitted. Eleanor knew that Rachel and Benjamin's relationship ended badly. He ended up quitting the shop after that. Neither one of them have spoken to him since.

"Only till someone gets back..." Eleanor muttered, into her wine glass. Rachel shot her an evil look.

"What is that supposed to mean?" She snapped, shoving popcorn into her mouth. Rachel had brought out almost all the snacks from Eleanor's pantry at that point.

"Well... I don't know. I thought maybe you had a thing for Ryan." Eleanor said with a shrug trying to play it cool.

Rachel sputtered. "You're kidding me right? I don't like the person that made my time in high school a living hell. He is one of the reasons why I left Hope Harbor and don't think I don't know what you're going to ask. Nothing happened that night just a lot of yelling, mostly from me. I just let him have what was building up all those years and you know what? It felt good, to finally put him in his place," she declared.

Eleanor noticed Rachel looked the opposite of good, but Eleanor wasn't going to pry anymore. She just nodded and added. "Good for you! I am sorry he did that to you."

"You know what...it has made me a stronger person. I realized life is too precious and I forgave him that night as well. So I guess we're fine. I just still don't like the man for more reasons than that, but that is for another bottle of wine," she smirked half-heartedly.

"This isn't good." Eleanor repeated, in her mind as she frantically drove to Ryan's parents' house after getting a call from his mother, who sounded distressed on the phone. A million thoughts raced through her mind, including the thoughts of Andrew in horrible scenarios. She pounded at the door.

Owen opened up the door with a sweet smile on his face, even though his eyes were worn and tired. "She is in the den." He said as he showed her to the room. Ryan's mom, Olivia was watching the weather channel frantically as she held her phone in her hand.

"What's wrong?" Eleanor blurted, in a worried rush.

"Paul just called me on the satellite phone, Hurricane Kelly and is heading their way. They're trying their best to get to the closest harbor, but they believe it will hit them before they can," she stated trying to sound calm; probably hoping it would calm Eleanor's nerves that were now raging like the storm.

"Are they going to keep us updated?" Eleanor asked, her words rushing out. Olivia set her hands on top of Eleanor's.

"Yes, it will be okay. I am sorry for freaking you out over the phone. This has happened before and they were fine. I just overreact sometimes. I probably didn't help your nerves at all. Let's get away from the news and have some tea with Owen," she reassured Eleanor, continuing to hold her hand as they get up and head to the kitchen.

Eleanor ended up staying into the evening with Olivia and Owen. It was nice to be around loved ones. She even went and got Trevor so they could spend the night at the house with them at Olivia's request. They never received the call from Paul or anyone. They kept an eye on the weather, but it was hard to do without knowing their location.

When the sun began to rise, Eleanor was already awake with the storm that raged last night and her nerves going crazy, she was lucky if she got a couple hours of sleep. She sat in the sun room as she sipped on her coffee. She wondered if Olivia or anyone in the house for that matter got any sleep last night. She prayed a lot last night, which lately she had been doing more of. She just wanted Andrew home and safe, along with the rest of the crew. She couldn't and didn't want to imagine her life without him.

"Elle..." A male voice called, through the dining room. She got up to see her dad standing in the door way, looking like he had never slept last night at all. His face was white as a ghost's with dark circles under his eyes.

"Dad, oh my...are you okay? Please sit," she exclaimed, taking her dad's arm and urging him to sit on the sofa.

He avoided her eyes and stared down at his worn, dirty hands. He smelled of the sea and could tell his clothes were damp. "Dad, please...are you okay? What's wrong?"

This time after she asked, he looked up into her eyes and in that instant, she knew. He let out a deep sigh, taking both of her hands. She didn't want to hear what he had to say, she tried to hold back the avalanche of tears that were threatening to escape.

"It's Andrew...The ship didn't make it to the dock in time. Andrew and three others are missing. I have spent all night with the coast guard trying to look for them..." he stated almost in a whisper.

Her breathing and heart raced. She couldn't stop shaking her head, she dropped his hands, standing and started to pace the room as she raked her hands through her hair. She bit her lips to keep from crying, all she could think of was Andrew. She looked at her father's face and just lost it. She bolted from the back yard patio down the stairs to the private beach. Her bare feet pounded the wet sand and seashells pierced her feet. She didn't care...she headed toward the water. The arctic cold from the water hit her like a lightning strike. She went out until the water was up to her waist, were she let out the most sorrowful cry out into the watery abyss.

"You promised damn it! Andrew, come back to me...I love you!" she cried, out unto the ocean. Her worst nightmare had come true. Her heart was breaking into million pieces and was floating away in the breeze across the ocean like dust. Eleanor thought this couldn't be happening to her.

"Please, Andrew...I love you. I love you." she whispered, this time as tears cascaded down her cheeks like a waterfall.

Back on the shore she could hear people shout her name but she just ignored them. The pain of the water didn't bother her anymore and she welcomed it instead. That was the only feeling she would ever know anymore; pain. With that she took one more breath and then plunged into the cold wet darkness.

CHAPTER TWENTY-SEVEN

Andrew was convinced he was dead. His whole body felt like it was put through a wood chopper, and it didn't help that he couldn't stop shivering. He felt drenched to the bone and the cool Atlantic wind didn't help him either. He wasn't sure how long he was on the beach. He fought back the pain as he looked up and gazed across it. Pine trees hugged the coast line. Suddenly, he noticed movement farther down the beach. He knew him and another crew member fell into the frozen water as he tried to help him get his foot untangled from the pulley. It was a greenhorn and it was his first big trip. He was trying his best to prove to others how tough he was. Andrew couldn't think of his name, he couldn't think of anything except Eleanor. He swore he heard her as he sank lower into the darkness, piercing coldness surrounding him.

Whatever it was made him push through upward. As much as it hurt him and all he wanted to do was give up, he knew he couldn't, because of the family that was waiting for him.

He grunted as he pushed his body to stand up,

sinking into the sand. He wiped the sand off his face and tried to keep his balance. He took one step at a time as he came closer to the object that was still moving on the shore. Each step felt like his legs were made of cement.

Sure enough, it was the greenhorn that was rolling in the sand. Andrew's eyes went wide when he saw the blood. He dropped down to the boy and ripped his jeans to see a gash below his knee about six inches long. Andrew tried to calm the boy down who just gained consciousness and freaked when he saw his leg.

"Shh...it's okay, I got you. Let me fix this up and then we will figure out where we are," Andrew commented as he took the boys jeans that he ripped and tied it tight around the kid's leg, making him scream out in pain. Andrew grimaced, he couldn't imagine what pain the boy must be in, but the longer they stayed out there the worse it's was going to get.

He helped the kid up, putting most of his weight on him. "What is your name again?" Andrew asked, as he helped the kid onto a small boulder.

"It's Noah." He said through his teeth as he tried to hold in the pain.

"That's right! Okay Noah, what he need to do is to find a shelter then make a fire. See that rock ledge up ahead? I see a cave that we can use as shelter. So I need you to help me get you up there, can you do that?" Andrew asked. Noah didn't say anything but just nodded.

Half way up the rock ledge, Noah couldn't go on anymore. He was losing more blood and started to look pale. Without a second thought, Andrew hoisted Noah over both his shoulders and carried him the rest of the way. Once they were in the cave, Andrew set Noah down gently and changed his bandage. Andrew would have to find a way to bring the water to the cave, the salt in the water would help the wound get clean. Noah leaned against the rock face and fell asleep.

While he left Noah sleeping, he climbed back down the rock ledge to try and find some dry branches to start a fire. He found some dry brush and bigger sticks. It took him five trips to get all the wood on the ledge and by then he was thirsty as hell. That was his next order of business.

It took Andrew over an hour to start the fire, but once he got that first spark and it started to smoke, he wanted to get up and dance. The fire was blazing hot and bright. He dragged Noah, who was still groggy and half asleep, by the fire. After that, he brought up more wood that would hopefully get them through the night. Once that was done, he went back to the beach to find big enough shells for his next project. He noticed that the trees where dripping rain water from the previous storm. He figured he could catch enough rain water so Noah and he could have some fresh water to drink. While his mind was busy thinking of how to survive it also kept drifting back to Trevor and Eleanor. Word must have gotten out that he was missing and he couldn't imagine what they were going through.

Last night, the captain tried to sail the boat as close to shore as they could. But the storm traveled faster than anyone thought. Everything was going fine, but once the waves started to get rough, the crew did their best to try and tie everything down. That's when Noah's foot got caught in the pulley, as a giant wave crashed into the ship, throwing everyone across the width of the boat, but Noah was so close to the edge, he flew over. Andrew saw, and jumped toward Noah trying to grasp his jacket before he fell into the water, but he lost his balance and fell in with Noah into the icy abyss. All he could remember after that, was the darkness surrounding him and being so cold that his mind went frantic, until he heard her voice.

It took close to five hours just to get two shells that could fit about eight ounces of water for the both of them. He brought them up to Noah who was getting worse. Andrew was afraid that Noah wouldn't make it much longer. He lost a lot of blood and needed medical attention badly. He held Noah's head up, trying to get him to drink the water,

"Noah, you're going to get through this, I promise you. Just be strong. We will get out of here soon." Andrew was running out of options and he hadn't even gotten around to finding food. He just knew Noah was running out of time and couldn't stand it if the boy lost his life on his watch. He got Noah to drink, giving him all of his water and most of his own. Andrew was starting to get desperate. He didn't want to travel with Noah's leg, so he thought of the next best thing; a smoke signal. He didn't know if it would work, but he would be damned if he didn't try.

Four days had passed since her dad told her about Andrew. Eleanor didn't know what to do with herself and was surprised at how time flew by the past couple of days. She felt numb and her brain seemed to be in a fog. She couldn't think or act normal and she wasn't sure what to feel at all. She tried her best to show everyone she was being positive, but every minute that went by and Andrew didn't walk through the door she felt herself slowly dying a little more. Of course she stayed positive for Trevor, who surprisingly seemed to be the most optimistic out of everyone. He had no doubt that Andrew would be coming home soon.

Ryan and Paul hadn't arrived either but would be arriving home sometime today. She and Trevor hadn't left Ryan's parent's home since finding out about Andrew.

Amelia also stayed and most days Rachel would come over as well. She couldn't have asked for a better support group. Her father hadn't left her side either, except when he left this morning to go pick up Ryan and his dad from the airport. She couldn't help but hope with every fiber in her that Andrew would walk through the door laughing behind Ryan and Paul. The clock ticked more and more slowly as Eleanor parked herself in front of the fire place, with coffee in hand, and snuggled under an afghan. Her gaze kept going to the clock then to the door.

"Do you mind some company?" Rachel asked, coming in from the kitchen with her own coffee cup.

"Of course!" Eleanor smiled, taking a sip of her coffee. Eleanor felt the heat of the coffee swirl up, giving her face a nice glow. The coffee's aroma was a rich complex blend of caramel and chocolate with a hint of sea salt. Eleanor couldn't help but to keep smelling it, letting the scent wash through her. They were quiet for a while; both seemed to be lost in their thoughts. Rachel suddenly looked at Eleanor like she wanted to say something but whenever she opened her mouth nothing came out.

Eleanor smiled encouragingly at Rachel. Rachel has been a godsend to her. She wouldn't know what she would do without her and Amelia. "I don't know if I have said this to you, but thank you for everything. Your friendship and presence at this time has been an anchor through this storm." Eleanor smiled, grabbing Rachel's hand giving her a gentle squeeze.

Rachel smiled bright, her cheeks turning red. "Girl, I feel for some reason I was sent back to Hope Harbor to become friends with you. When we first met, something hit me and made me think- I need this woman. I don't know why or how but she is going to be someone important in my life. I feel as if we're sisters from another mister," she said with a small giggle. "But seriously...you mean the world to me."

Eleanor set down her mug at the same time Rachel did and embraced each other in a tight hug. Eleanor could feel the love and friendship emitting from. It gave Eleanor some belief that everything was going to work out in the end. She didn't know how long they hugged each other but when they finally let go, both were teary-eyed.

Owen walked into the room, shocked at their expressions, "Did I interrupt something?"
He asked, concerned look crossing his face.

Eleanor and Rachel both laughed and shook their heads. "No, we're just having a nice talk. Would you like to join us?" Rachel asked, picking her cup back up, taking a sip.

His expression changed from concern to excitement, "I would but Paul and Ryan just pulled up in the drive way. I came to see if you guys wanted to come out and join us in greeting them," he asked, waiting for them both to get up which wasn't long. Eleanor and Rachel jumped up when he told them, almost spilling their coffee.

Owen let them go first through the kitchen out to the side deck where the garage was. They both waited on the deck, Eleanor's body hummed. She prayed over and over in her head, "Please let Andrew be in the car." The car drove up where they could peer through the windows. Eleanor was confused because her father wasn't driving the car, someone from the boat was. She noticed Paul was in the passenger seat and her heart dropped when she only saw one person in the back.

Ryan's mother rushed out to the car, scuffling her slippers along the gravel to the passenger side of the vehicle. She gave Paul a fierce hug as tears rolled down her cheeks. Paul shook his head and smiled as he hugged his wife. "I told you everything would be okay," he reassured her. She did a little laugh sob, then let Paul go and rushed to Ryan who had barely gotten out of the car before she ambushed him. She couldn't see their interaction but she could hear Ryan's voice say over and over. "Mom, I'm okay...I'm okay."

Owen was the next one by the car, giving his son and grandson hugs. Eleanor was ecstatic they were back, but couldn't help having a small pang of jealousy that they were back and not Andrew. Once the family was done were their embraces, Paul and Ryan made it up onto the porch where Ryan set down his duffle bag and took Eleanor in his arms, lifting her off the ground in a fierce hug. She gripped him tighter not wanting to let him go. Ever since Andrew and Eleanor had been together she felt Ryan was one of her dearest friends and big brother.

"Don't give up Eleanor, I promise you he will be home," he whispered in her ear. All she could do was nod.

"Thank you," she choked out, giving him one more squeeze before he set her down.

When they pulled away she noticed his gaze wasn't toward her but toward Rachel. Rachel's cheeks flushed but neither one spoke, until Rachel sighed and smiled. "It's good to see you home Ryan," she said, as she placed her hand on his arm giving him a slight squeeze.

Ryan seemed to be fighting an internal battle of some kind because emotions from angry, to sad, to happy flashed across his face. He nodded and said. "Thank you."

Eleanor couldn't help but gawk at the interaction between the two. She could sense the tension and endearment to one another. The heat between them could give you sunburn. Rachel blushed realizing she had his arm and quickly dropped her hand. He glanced at her a moment longer and then headed inside. Her face still red, she looked down, set her coffee on the deck railing and left the porch. Eleanor wanted to go after her friend but she knew Rachel wouldn't want to talk about it. Rachel would tell her in time.

"Where is my father?" Eleanor asked after everything settled down and Eleanor, Owen, Paul, and Ryan were in the kitchen. Ryan's mother was napping in the living room.

"He had some business in town and was going to show up later tonight," Paul stated, taking a swig of his beer. Eleanor nodded but was confused that her father didn't call and tell her. She figured he must have got caught up in something and lost track of time.

After supper, Eleanor decided to head down to the beach to clear her thoughts. She sat on a big boulder and stared out into the vast, watery abyss, wondering where Andrew could be; if he was okay, or even alive. Every beat of her heart seemed like a drum of war, pounding throughout her body. It was almost was as loud as the ocean. It seemed her body wanted to broadcast it for Andrew to hear. When she saw that man again, she vowed to never let him go or be out of her sight.

The wind began to pick up and she felt a strange turn in the air. She couldn't explain it but it felt electrifying. She turned to look out at the beach when her breath caught in her throat, farther down the beach, stood a figure. Every bone in her body knew that man...Andrew. She jumped down on the rock. Stones poked her feet, stinging a little, but she couldn't care less. She began to run in the wet sand that made it hard for her feet to move. The man saw her and began to run toward her. As they got closer and closer Eleanor pushed faster and faster till she saw his tired and worn, but jubilant face. He had cuts on his chiseled cheek bones that were covered with a well grown beard. At first glance he was almost unrecognizable. They got close enough where Andrew's energy ran out and he fell to his knees. Eleanor fell to her knees and into his arms. He grabbed her and touched her all over, as if to see if she was real. Eleanor did the same and made sure he wasn't hurt.

"Oh Andrew!" She gasped as he pulled her into a tight hug, rocking back and forth on their knees.

He pulled away and wiped her tears. "I'm here. I'm here and I will never leave you again," He paused and looked deep into her eyes. "I love you Eleanor, I heard you. I heard your prayers. Please say you will be mine forever. Will you marry me?" Andrew poured out his soul.

Eleanor smiled brightly and sweetly. "I have traveled a thousand miles to find myself and I found more than I ever thought possible. I love you Andrew...Yes, I will," she said sealing her vow and her promise with a kiss.

The End